Begin Again

Lori Bell

https://www.emedicine.medscape.com
https://www.passiongrowers.com/roses

Printed by CreateSpace

ISBN 978 1977898753

DEDICATION

To my son, Connor. In so many ways, you have taught me to
begin again.

Chapter one

The abrupt tapping on her car window startled Poppy Brennan from her sleep. She gripped the steering wheel in front of her and darted her eyes to her left. Through the sealed, partially fogged window she saw the ferry tenant in his fluorescent orange vest. She barely heard his voice on the other side of the glass. "Your turn lady! Pull up as close as you can to the vehicle in front of you. It's time to drive off the dock." She had reached her destination. Martha's Vineyard.

Forty minutes ago, when she parked her silver sedan on the ferry's dock, Poppy didn't want to get out of her car. She just turned off the engine and put her head back against the seat. She intended to only close her eyes for a few minutes. The air was chilly, so she hadn't cracked a single window in her car. And now, those fogged windows annoyed her as she inched off the dock and turned the defrost on full blast.

The commute from where she lived in Boston to Martha's Vineyard was less than three hours but, even still, Poppy felt drained as she made it to Oak Bluffs, which was one of the six towns located on the ninety-six miles of island. The cottage on the beach still looked the same as it did when Poppy was a young girl. Her last memory of it was when she was twelve. The sky blue siding and wraparound porch with white railing remained a staple. The windows, sans panes, were etched in Poppy's memory. She remembered her mother opening wide all of those windows each time they arrived on island in the spring or summertime. There were no screens so when the wind picked up on the water and along the beach, sand habitually blew in. Poppy still recalled the feel of the grit on the bottom of her bare feet after she padded through the living room.

It wasn't summertime now, it was late November and the fifty-four degree air temperature was chilly but comfortable, Poppy thought. Poppy's family and a few friends, who were aware she had packed up to spend infinite time at the cottage on the island, had all spoken the same. *Isn't that a summer colony? The businesses must be boarded up! What will you do there all winter long?* Not to mention both of her daughters had asked her if she was certain she wanted to revisit *that* place.

That was just it. What did it matter to anyone what she would do there, or anywhere, all winter long? Poppy was tired of the loneliness in her Boston townhouse. It was too much for just one person. The space. The silence. Her life as she knew it had changed *too much* in the last six months. Change had eaten away at her soul. And here she was, about to make yet another alteration to her life.

The welcome mat was sun-bleached and worn under the flip flops on her feet as Poppy wheeled her full-size suitcase up to the door. The key, unfailingly kept underneath the mat through the years, was already in Poppy's hand. But now that she was truly there, Poppy began to question her decision. A decision that was so impromptu she barely had given herself time to pack her belongings. She didn't bring much from her Boston townhouse, only what she could fit into a suitcase and several other things were still in the trunk of her car. The key she now held in her hand prompted her to just do it. *Go inside.* She had made it this far. Back there. Back to the cottage. After all these years.

She turned the key and pushed open the door. She purposely distracted herself with looking down at her luggage and rolling it over the threshold. The smell was familiar. A little musty. She could envision her mother throwing open the windows now, one after another. There were three medium-size windows facing the front of the house, the Atlantic Ocean view. It was a ritual. The very first thing her mother did every single time when they arrived on Martha's Vineyard.

She noticed the distinct scent of Pine Sol now. Just a few days ago, Poppy had left a voicemail for the caretaker to ready the house. She wondered afterward if that recording had gone unheard and if she would arrive on island to cobwebs and dust bunnies. That would not have been so awful. Poppy wasn't too proud or proper to clean. It was nice, however, to see the old wood flooring had been mopped and the furniture was unveiled from underneath the white sheets that covered the sofa and chairs when the cottage was vacant. Covering the furniture had been Poppy and her little brother's job as children. On the last day of their island stay, they were instructed to get the freshly washed and dried sheets out of the dryer and *cover up the cushions*. Poppy could still recall the warmth of the sheets against her skin as she carried them to the living room to wrap the furniture. *Tuck the corners*. Her brother never did. *Leave it to Bobby*.

Poppy took a closer look around the room now. Some of the tension, stemming from where she was, had begun to subside. Her eyes were now able to focus on the detail in the room. The walls were painted mint green. The furniture was different. It wasn't new, because it looked worn. But it was new to Poppy. Gone were the pastel floral printed sofa and matching loveseat from the early 1970s. Had Poppy really expected that furniture to still be there? She was fifty-three years old now — and back then she was a child. There was now a white suede sofa and two matching recliner chairs placed in the middle of the room where a wagon wheel glass-topped coffee table was the center point. The lines on the white furniture had appeared brush-like or possibly a vacuum had been run over them. Poppy never did like suede. Who wants to see every little marking of where they, or somebody else, had been? She had to admit though, white was a striking look for that room. It made everything seem brighter. More inviting. There was still a tube television set, the console kind, which Poppy remembered well.

She wondered if it even worked. It really didn't matter. She never cared much for watching television. She would just read, or walk the beach. She prepared ahead and packed a few jackets, even her heaviest winter down.

Poppy walked toward the front windows. The wooden wide-paneled white blinds were entirely open. She could see the ocean. She allowed herself to look now. It was within steps from her. This cottage used to be their dream place. Poppy hadn't allowed herself to miss it, and she certainly hadn't dared to come back. This place was a part of her past that she always kept tucked away. Until now.

She peered through the open blinds, down the beach, and near the water. She spotted something red. She squinted her eyes. The sun wasn't allowing her to focus on exactly what it was. And perhaps her eyesight wasn't what it used to be. Poppy left the window and made her way over to open the door. She walked outside in her black flip flops, wide legged denim, and a black waffle-knit sweater with a flat hood against her back and two drawstrings hanging on her chest. She stepped off of the boardwalk that led up to the cottage. Her feet were sinking in the sand, just as they had been earlier on her way up to the cottage from her car. The sun was bright and it should have warmed her, but instead the cool air chilled her. Poppy used her hand to form a visor over her eyes, as she stepped toward the ocean. Her strides were slow, but she was doing it. She was making it. She just didn't want to dwell on it right now. There was a fishing dock nearby, and that's where she had spotted something red from her window. Poppy felt a little foolish now as she realized she wasn't alone out there. There was a man, sitting on the dock, wearing a red baseball cap. She wanted to be alone out there, especially now. Poppy immediately thought about turning around and going back. But there was something about the man who made her stare longer. He couldn't see her, as his back was to her. His knees were pulled up to his chest. His arms and legs were covered in a jacket and denim, but his feet were bare. He sat next to a tackle box and a fishing pole, both were untouched. Poppy watched him stare at the ocean. Poppy was certain that massive body of water would have thousands of stories to tell, if it could throw back the thoughts and feelings people sent out to it. Sitting alone. Walking alone. The beach and the ocean waves were a therapeutic draw.

Poppy crossed her arms over her chest. It was chillier near the water. Her flip flops felt heavy in the sand and the bottoms of her flared denim were sweeping the white granules as she took steps. The steps back to her cottage. She would return out there, even closer to the water, later. When she was undoubtedly alone.

She never did anything to draw attention to herself. He must have sensed someone was there, or turned to leave also. And that's when he saw her on the beach. "Mrs. Brennan?"

Poppy hadn't answered to that name in years. Possibly when her children were in school? Maybe when her daughters introduced her to new boyfriends brought home from college, and she had been quick to tell them to *just call her Poppy.*

She turned. He stood on the dock, staring back at her. He apparently knew who she was. He waved his hand in the air, and then stepped off of the dock, into the sand.

Poppy squinted and used her hand again to shield her eyes from the merciless sun. She could almost hear her mother reminding her to *wear sunglasses, squinting will give you wrinkles.*

"Mrs. Brennan?" The man in the red cap asked again as he reached her. He had left his gear behind on the dock.

"Yes, I'm Poppy," she offered. "And you are?"

"Dudley Connors. You called me...to get the cottage ready. I hope it's to your liking?"

"You're the caretaker? Oh, I see. Yes, it's perfect. Thank you." Poppy had not done more than step inside the door and into the living room, where her suitcase on wheels was still parked. It didn't matter to her though. Spotless or not, the cottage had already begun to feel welcoming. Sort of like home. Home from many years ago.

When Poppy dialed the number for the caretaker of the cottage, she had not known who she was calling for. She had no name to request if someone answered the phone when she called and only left a voice message. Forty-something years ago a man and his wife, *the Brandmeyers,* Poppy remembered, were the couple who tended to the cottage for her grandparents. Poppy wondered if Mr. Connors was related to them.

"The number you called was my cell. Please use it if you need anything during your stay," he offered, and Poppy could see his brown hair graying around the ears, below his cap. "I was going to check on you tomorrow once you were settled in." He saw her car pull up and watched her drag her suitcase through the sand. There was something solemn in her body language then, and he identified it again now as she stood before him. She was no longer shielding her eyes from the sun that was now blocked by a moving cloud. Her arms were crossed over her chest. Her shoulder-length brown hair was blowing relentlessly and she made little effort to push it away from her face. The wind took her hair from every which direction. It was as if she didn't want to make the effort to fight it. Dudley watched this, and he had gotten a quick glimpse at her sad brown eyes.

"Thank you. I just got in. I haven't even unpacked. The beach was calling my name, I guess." Poppy felt a sudden pang as she spoke those words. It was actually her curiosity for the red splotch in the distance that rushed her out there, which was now the snug-fitting cap on this man's head.

"It's a little chilly for a beach day," he shrugged.

"But not too chilly for fishing?" she asked him and he caught a slight smile from her face.

"No fishing for me. I'm supposed to be, but I'm not," he offered, and Poppy didn't follow him. Nor did she question him.

"Well, it was nice to meet you. Doug?" She was trying to wrap up this unexpected encounter.

"Dudley," he corrected.

"Right, sorry," Poppy said.

"No worries, Poppy." He liked her name, and she felt a little embarrassed that he had remembered hers, but she had botched his.

He watched her walk away. He shouldn't have been staring. If she would have turned back around to glance over her shoulder, his face would have reddened to match his cap. He couldn't help it though. She seemed so sad.

Poppy told herself not to look back at least three times as she walked up the beach to the short boardwalk that led to the wraparound porch. She could feel him watching her. *Or maybe it was her imagination?* She would see him again. She probably should have asked how much she owed him for getting the cottage ready for her. She would next time, or he would just bill her, she thought, as she closed the door behind her and slipped off her sand-coated flip flops on the floor.

Her toes were painted cherry red, like Dudley's cap. She didn't bother brushing the sand off of them as she padded bare foot across the living room floor. She made her way into the kitchen. It was somewhat like she remembered. The matching white appliances were long replaced. Stainless steel was in now. She walked to the refrigerator and expected to find it empty when she opened the door. There was bottled water and white wine. Poppy smirked. *Bobby.* She remembered when she and her brother were eleven and twelve years old and they had figured out how to unscrew the cork on a wine bottle that either their parents or grandparents had intended to drink. The two of them drank the entire bottle. *Bobby initiated it, it was his idea,* Poppy recalled, and then she caught herself smiling again. This time with tears welling up in her eyes. *White wine had been her favorite ever since.*

She bent forward and retrieved the bottle. She held it by the neck as she closed the refrigerator door and opened two cabinets before she found the glasses. There were a half a dozen stemless wine glasses. She took one. This particular bottle had a twist cap. *Some things in life were easier now.*

After her first sip, Poppy sat down at the round kitchen table. It was the very same table, from forty-plus years ago. It seemed smaller. But she was sure it was the one. The wood surface was scratched and worn in spots. The chair she sat on was the same as then too. It was after Poppy sat down when she realized she was the third generation woman to sit at that table, there in the cottage. Her grandmother. Her mother. And now her. But she wasn't a little girl anymore. She was fifty-three years old. She had crow's feet and laugh lines. Her breasts weren't as perky as they once were. Her size ten, five-seven frame was still curvy, but love handles were permanent now. Poppy took aging with ease. She was grateful for every year earned. She lived through both trying and effortless times, and Poppy persevered with grace and poise through all of them. It was after she turned twelve that Poppy realized life was precious and she had better live every day. Before it was taken away.

Poppy took a long sip of her wine before she set the glass down on the tabletop in front of her, and closed her eyes. It was the summer's end of 1976. She and Bobby, along with their mother, were leaving the cottage. Their father had stayed behind in Boston to work. He had only visited there two weekends during the entire summer.

The furniture was covered. The place had been cleaned. They were leaving it just as they found it. The door was now locked. Their mother took off walking three cottages down, to give her final payment to the caretaker. Poppy could still see her, those tight dark brown permed curls on her head, with her purse on her arm, practically marching through the sand, down the beach. And a moment later, Bobby spotted the cocker spaniel too close to the water. It was the puppy from the cottage next door. The family brought the dog with them that summer, and Bobby had gotten so attached to it that all he did was beg their mother for a dog just like Timmy for when they returned home to Boston. Their mother was adamant in her refusal. She wasn't a dog person. Bobby had cried.

And then Poppy witnessed the worry on his face, the fear in his voice, when he darted off through the sand to save Timmy from the current. At first, Poppy didn't see the harm. Bobby was a fantastic swimmer. He would rescue the dog — unfamiliar to the ocean water — and be a hero. Bobby was always doing things of the sort to make their parents beam with pride. Poppy never denied she had the perfect little brother. So close in age, they could have been twins, even though Bobby was a head shorter than her and had a mop of blond hair in contrast to Poppy's long dark hair. If anything, they were certainly as emotionally close as twins.

Bobby, nor the little dog, ever surfaced in the ocean that day. Poppy opened her eyes now, but she could still see the red baseball cap her brother was wearing that awful day as it thrashed between the rough waves of the ocean, and then sunk too deep, and so abruptly washed out to sea.

Chapter two

Poppy was day drinking, and she never gave it a second thought. It was this place. The ironic fact that there was a bottle of white wine in the refrigerator. Poppy needed to honor Bobby's memory. Finally, she returned to the cottage to face the pain of her past. And also because she wanted to escape what was left of her life in Boston.

After Bobby drowned, Poppy remembered going back to Boston to a life she no longer recognized. Her father, the workaholic judge for the Boston Municipal Court, was lost to them. He threw himself even deeper into his career. Even as a child, Poppy had been able to identify how her parents failed at grieving, and fell short at moving on. During a moment of her rebellious teenage years, Poppy had lashed out at her mother, making the mere point of how she had lost both of her parents, too, the day that her brother died! Her mother slapped her hard across the face and told her she never wanted to hear those words from her again. *Denial.*

It wasn't until her mother was on her death bed, just six months ago, when she whispered the words, *I'm sorry. I'm sorry I failed you when God took our Bobby away from us. You deserved so much more than I was capable of giving you after your brother was gone.* Poppy had only taken her mother's frail, wrinkled hand, and gently held it. She could have said *it's okay,* or something of comfort in response, but the words never came. Probably because it wasn't okay.

Poppy's father died at the age of sixty eight of a heart attack in his chambers, following a regular court appearance. Her mother died, twelve years after, at the age of eighty, from congestive heart failure. Poppy saw the irony of their causes of death. Both of their hearts were broken and never again had been able to pulse quite up to par after the death of their little boy.

Losing her parents had not destroyed her. Poppy had been invincible and strong all of her adult life. Being raised by two oftentimes callous parents had made her feel capable of overcoming hardship. The love of one man had also kept her going and happy for a very long time. Reed Brennan had given her twenty-eight years of something of her own. A marriage, which she compared as much healthier and happier than she witnessed her parents having. Children, two daughters, which she commended herself for raising so unlike her mother had her. There was open communication, trust, and unconditional love in their family. Or so she believed.

Looking back, Poppy wondered how she could have missed the signs. Her husband was an oral surgeon. He was a busy man. He got called away on emergencies. When she thought back now, Poppy no longer trusted any one time he rushed off in a hurry to help someone. *A child knocked out her two front teeth when she flipped over the handlebars of her bicycle. A man busted out an eye tooth when a power drill malfunctioned in his hands.* None of it, fact or fabrication, held merit or mattered anymore.

Three months ago, Poppy had walked into her husband's den on the main level of their townhouse. She saw him poring over a newspaper article. She noticed the tears on his face. She asked him what was wrong, but he brushed her off and hid that section of the newspaper underneath the clutter on his desktop. He changed the subject then, but Poppy had not let it go from her mind. She wanted to know what he had been reading in the newspaper when she walked in on him. Reed was hardly an overly sensitive man, but something had obviously touched him.

A part of her wished she had never gone back into the den later to rummage through the stash of papers. But she had. And the fact remained that an obituary for a woman a decade younger than her was of interest to her husband. She felt like a spy, a private investigator, or a damn good detective. When he made the mistake of wearing his solid black funeral tie to work the next day, Poppy got into her car and followed him. He never said he was going to a visitation or a memorial, but that's where Poppy had trailed him. She expected him to get in line, a wait that looked to be terribly long when Poppy stepped through the door of the funeral home. She stayed back and didn't glance around, in fear of making eye contact with someone she knew. She put out of her mind how she was dressed down, just wearing a pair of dark-washed denim with a black turtle neck and black ballet flats on her bare feet. At least she had worn black today, unbeknownst to where she was going. She was on a mission there — inside of that sterile, eerie building — to go after her husband, not to out-dress or make conversation. And besides, what would she say if she had been asked her connection to the newly deceased?

Reed cut in line, or so it appeared he had. Poppy stretched her neck to see more. It was as if the receiving line had stopped for him. She saw him step up close to the casket, lean into it, and over the woman's lifeless body inside. His shoulders shook, but Poppy was too far away to hear if he was sobbing. *What did he care about that dead woman?* Poppy stepped out of line and inched closer to this confusing scene. She could feel eyes on her as she walked, but she didn't care. She reached a few feet from the casket before she stopped. There was a young man there, barely twenty years old. She watched him wrap a strong, loving arm around Reed, as both of them stood directly in front of the casket. Poppy had a full view of that young man. He was every bit as tall as Reed's six-foot-two height. His hair was full and wavy and a familiar dark brown, just as Reed's had been when Poppy met him for the first time. His shoulders were broad. His waist was narrow. It was strange for Poppy to look at him, but she couldn't stop staring. Puzzlement filled her mind. *Who was that boy? And why was her husband here?*

In just minutes, after Reed would spot his wife behind him, he would escort her outside and give in to her demands and regretfully confess out on the rainy street in front of the funeral home how that young man was his son. He had an ongoing affair with the woman who had been killed in a car accident just three days prior. Poppy's husband had lived a double life. For two decades of their twenty-eight years together, he had a mistress. And with her, he had conceived and raised a son. *Poppy's husband had another family.*

She poured herself a second glass of white wine. Coming back to the cottage after all these years was something she needed to do. It hadn't mattered though, whether Poppy was in Boston or on Martha's Vineyard, she still felt like a book falling off its binding. It was the most isolated, helpless feeling she had experienced in a very long time.

✦ ✦ ✦

Her cell phone, tucked inside of the outer pocket of her suitcase, was ringing. The silence in that cottage, where Poppy was alone with only her thoughts, was broken by a ringtone.

Poppy stood up and felt the rush of the alcohol to her head. Two glasses. She inhaled deeply through her nostrils as she walked swiftly into the living room to see who was trying to reach her — and if she even wanted to answer the call.

It was Reed, and she knew she didn't want to talk to him. Other than their divorce proceedings, they had barely spoken to each other after that day on the curb outside of the funeral home. Well, Reed had undoubtedly spoken. He begged for her forgiveness. He pleaded for a second chance. But all of his words and emotions had not entered Poppy's cold, broken heart. She asked him to do for her one last thing. Divorce her. Sign the papers. She no longer wanted to call him her husband, and she certainly couldn't stand the thought of remaining as his wife.

They were no longer married. No longer sharing a house, meals, a bed. Three months already spent living apart after unimaginable heartbreak, and then one piece of paper had severed their bond. But time and space thus far hadn't erased twenty-eight years of love and memories. Poppy didn't want to forget, but she also wouldn't allow herself to remember. She wasn't ready to rehash anything about what she had thought was hers and hers alone. Her husband. The father of only her children. Reed Brennan had deceived her and embarrassed her in the worst possible way. Even still, she answered his call. "Hello?"

"Poppy! Good, you answered. Are you on island?" Reed spoke as if he still had a right to her. And Poppy was both unnerved and touched. It was going to take time for the effect he had on her to subside. If it ever would.

"I'm at the cottage, yes," she answered him.

She heard him sigh on the opposite end. "That cannot be easy. You shouldn't be there alone."

"But I am alone now, Reed. We're divorced." It was as if Poppy enjoyed reminding him, and Reed loathed knowing he was caught and suffered the fallout. He had lost both women he loved. What would eventually kill him, he knew, was when Poppy opened her heart to someone else. It would happen. She was a beautiful woman who had aged so gracefully through the years he almost felt jealous. Why had only his hair thinned and his waistline thickened? Poppy would catch the eye of another man for sure. She was good and pure, kind and loving. Making love to her had always been as soothing as light rain on a rooftop. Being with her was comfortable. She was home for him. And then there was another woman. She was a thunderstorm with hard rains and wild winds. Hurricane status. She rocked his world and Reed never had been strong enough to leave her.

"I still care, you know. I'll tell the girls you're safe and sound at the cottage."

"The girls can call me themselves anytime. They're yours and mine now, not ours." *And you have a son too. You always have. Bastard. How badly for a period of time in their lives Poppy had wanted to give him a son. Having another child, three children, had not been out of the question for them.*

"They're the best of us, Poppy. That can't be denied or erased."

"Then go spend time with your daughters, Reed. And as for me, I'll be fine."

"I know you will," she heard him say before he ended the call.

While she held her cell phone in her hand, Poppy checked for other messages. She had three texts. The first was from her youngest daughter, Tealy. Tealy lived in Boston, just eight miles from Poppy's and Reed's townhouse — which was now just Poppy's home. Tealy was married to a stockbroker and had three small children, two girls, five and three years old, and a baby boy, eighteen months old. Tealy had gone to college for a business degree, but she had stated time and again that all she wanted to be when she grew up was a mother. So Poppy believed her baby girl was living her dream. The text read, *Mom— I'm sure you're at the cottage by now. Go easy on yourself there. If it's too much, come home.* Poppy smiled. What exactly was too much? Her life, in general, had felt like too much these last few months.

The second text was from her ex-husband. Reed had naturally followed up by contacting her with a phone call. He was impatient in that way. His text, two hours prior, had read, *Thinking about you. Worried you're setting yourself up for pain. Call me. Or, at least text a reply so I know you made it safely.* Setting herself up for pain? Poppy actually laughed out loud, but then her voice caught in her throat. She still felt like crying over that man. The man she gave her life to was the one who certainly *caused her pain.*

The third text was from her oldest daughter. Poppy was most surprised by her message. Most of the contact between her and her thirty-one-year-old daughter was initiated by Poppy. CeCe was independent, successful, and always a free spirit. She was dedicated to her career as a video producer and director. She was not married, and claimed she never dated seriously. Her message to Poppy was short and to the point, *Tealy told me you're probably on island by now. It's about time, if you ask me. Peace.* Poppy grinned, nodded her head, and thought, *Yeah, I sure hope I can find the peace that I'm looking for.*

Poppy turned off her cell phone without responding to any of her messages. They all knew where she was. Now they could leave her alone.

Chapter three

While it was still daylight on the island, Poppy gathered her handbag and car keys and left the cottage. She needed groceries. The complimentary wine and water in the refrigerator would not keep her alive forever. She was going to drive into the downtown area of Oak Bluffs and go to the market.

The people were friendly there, which was something Poppy really had not picked up on as a child. She remembered their time at the cottage as being about family. Her grandparents often stayed there with Poppy, her mother, and Bobby — and occasionally her father. She also recalled befriending other families who rented the cottages along the beach for the summer. When she was twelve, which was the last summer they had come to Martha's Vineyard after Bobby had tragically drowned, Poppy had a crush on the fourteen-year-old boy who was staying two cottages down. She would play Frisbee on the beach with him, and they fished together off of the dock. Once, the sun had been setting and Poppy knew she had to get back to the cottage. They were sitting close together on the dock, dangling their feet over. Kirk was his name, and he had teased Poppy about not yet being a teenager. *He was already in his second year, and she was just a kid.* Poppy was hardly a kid. She had blossomed early. Her breasts were no longer just buds. Her body was curvy. Her waistline was narrow. Her rear had filled out her bikini perfectly. Poppy remembered that boy so vividly. Sun-bleached hair. His bangs hung in his eyes. His chest was broad. His suntanned abs were something she could stare at for hours. She hadn't dared to touch him though. He was the first to touch her. He held her face in both of his hands as he leaned into her and kissed her. Poppy's first kiss was magical. Kirk had obviously done that before. He was gentle and tender and she willingly and awkwardly met his lips and then her tongue with his. The kiss was one to remember. Poppy had left the island that summer a changed girl. She was beginning to feel like a woman, but the thrill of the chase to become one had been halted when she lost her little brother.

Poppy was thinking about her first kiss now as she wondered where in the world that boy named Kirk may have ended up. Hopefully he had a wife on the receiving end of his magical kisses. She laughed to herself. Sometimes memories weren't all they were cracked up to be. That, however, was one Poppy felt compelled to hold onto. It was her way of still believing in romance and love. Now, especially.

As Poppy drove to the cottage with a backseat cargo of fresh fruit, vegetables, and seafood, she thought of Reed. Their marriage had felt solid. She did more than her part to raise their girls, while Reed focused on his career as an oral surgeon and provided very well for their family. Poppy had once been just like her youngest daughter, Tealy. All she ever wanted was to raise babies. Many of Poppy's female friends through the years came and went in her life. She never had a really close relationship with another woman. The times she had bonded with girlfriends in various stages of her life, Poppy could remember laughs and intimate conversations. Many of the women had great sex lives, while a few complained and stated they could live without it. Poppy never chimed in with anything too personal. She had not felt close enough to another woman to confess that she had not ever truly yearned for the act of sex. She had lost her virginity in college in her dorm room. She and her roommate's brother had too much to drink one night when he was in town visiting. His sister had gone out for an impromptu date, and Poppy had gotten drunk with the boy she had just met. It was amicable. It was more about Poppy's curiosity, and deep down she had just wanted to un-label herself as a virgin. It was over as quickly as it started on the top bunk. Poppy had winced when he stuck his finger inside of her first. And just when she began to relax and enjoy the feeling from the repetitive rhythm of a boy's stiff penis inside of her, it had been over.

Poppy had slept with three boyfriends in the following years before she met Reed. Only one of those young men had given her genuine, full blown orgasms. Early in their relationship and in the beginning years of their marriage, Reed strived to please her in bed. Sometimes he succeeded. Many times their love making felt rushed. Poppy wondered now if she could pinpoint an instance when they were eight years into their marriage with two children —ages five and three— when Reed had strayed. They still made love, year after year, but if Poppy really thought about it now, she would admit their intimacy had changed. He barely touched her before he would thrust inside of her. He on occasion took his time as if he was savoring her, she believed, but it was as if he was already spent for foreplay or real affection. Now she knew his sexual energy had been exerted in another woman's bed. Time and again. Year after year.

What hurt Poppy the most was she missed her best friend. She was middle aged and then some, and she no longer thought too much about having a physical relationship. It was a comfortable part of their union but, to Poppy, their marriage had been about something bigger than sharing a bed. They shared a life. Love. Children. Memories. And, of course, it all now felt like a lie. A betrayal. Poppy was a divorced woman who, in so many ways, had to begin again.

She attempted to carry three grocery bags all at once. It was a feat she mastered when her children were little. The more she was able to juggle in one trip from the car in the garage, the quicker she made it into the house. She always had other things to do. The funny thing was now she had all of the time in the world. And she really didn't like that feeling at all.

The paper handle on one of the bags tore as she stepped onto the boardwalk in front of her cottage. Poppy caught the bag on her knee, and then she was startled to look up and see that red baseball cap again. Dudley, the caretaker, was there.

"Whoa," he said, hurrying to step toward her and take one of the bags from her. "You must make it all in one trip, huh?" he smiled. "My wife, um, well she used to do that all of the time." His smile faded.

Poppy saw the change in his expression just now, but she didn't know him well enough, or at all, to ask him to elaborate. *Where was his wife now? Was he divorced, too?*

"Yes, exactly," she replied. "I don't know why I'm in such a hurry. I have what feels like infinite time here." This time Dudley wondered why she was alone there, and without a plan. *Would someone be meeting her there? A husband? A lover?* She wasn't wearing a ring on her left hand.

Dudley stepped aside for Poppy to get to her cottage, but not before he relieved her of another grocery bag in her arms. "I came by, I knocked, and was just now going to leave. I wanted to see if you needed anything from uptown. I see you are pretty self-sufficient."

"Oh my gosh, I would never expect you to run my errands," Poppy said, as she stepped inside and he started to follow her, but stopped on the threshold.

"May I?" he asked, in mid step.

"Yes, of course, come in." This did feel awkward, inviting a stranger into the cottage where she was staying alone, but Poppy quickly reminded herself that Dudley had already been there. He blew out the dust bunnies and shined the floors. And probably scrubbed the toilet too.

Dudley nearly bumped into her suitcase in the walkway, but he dodged it at the last second. "Still haven't settled in?"

"Not yet," she answered, looking back as she walked into the kitchen and he followed. He was right. She had not unpacked or even begun to settle in. She still had the trunk of her car full of things she wanted to bring inside too. That was why she had to use the backseat for groceries when she left the market.

"So how long are you planning to stay?" Dudley asked, primarily just to make conversation, but he was working for her as well and thought he should have a general idea.

"I don't really know," she answered as she set one bag of groceries down on the small kitchen table, and Dudley followed her lead with the next two. Three bottles of white wine clanged together as Poppy reached inside the bag, took those bottles out one by one, and stood them upright on the table.

"Glad to see white wine was a good choice," he chuckled.

"Oh?" Poppy realized it was his doing. "Yes, it's my favorite. My family's favorite for generations, actually. So, you were the one who stocked my fridge?"

"I'd hardly call a bottle of wine and some water stocked, but yes," he smiled. Poppy laughed. Under the red ball cap, he had gorgeous hazel eyes. The scruff on his face was something else she hadn't noticed before either. He was wearing the same gray jacket and faded denim as earlier when she spotted him on the dock. This time he had brown leather flip flops on his feet. Poppy was still in her same clothes and flip flops as well.

He saw her staring and he looked down at his own feet. "I think I tracked in some serious sand."

"You and me both, and it's really totally fine. It's one of my most vivid memories from summers spent here actually. The place wouldn't feel the same if I wasn't walking around on gritty floors." She smiled again.

"So this isn't your first rodeo? Staying here, I mean."

"This cottage is family-owned. First by my grandparents, and then my parents. My mother died six months ago. I had not given coming to this cottage, and definitely not its ownership, a serious thought in many years. Then I found out it was willed to me."

"I'm sorry about your loss," he offered. "It's been empty here for awhile. A man by the name of Van stayed last summer." He was Poppy's cousin on her mother's side of the family. Van was married three times and thrice divorced. He had probably entertained a woman there. Poppy felt like rolling her eyes, but at least he was putting the cottage to use. Her mother had never shared that information with her. Poppy wondered who else she had given permission to stay. Someone in the family had updated the cottage's décor a little over the years.

"Well it's only going to be me to come and go for awhile." Poppy wasn't really sure why she had said *go.* She had no intention of returning to Boston anytime soon.

"Then I should welcome you here, officially." Dudley reached out his hand. Poppy's cheeks flushed. She felt a nervous flutter in her belly as she reached out her hand in response and he gently took it. "The island is a beautiful place. I hope you will be very comfortable here."

"Thank you. I do, too," Poppy removed her hand from his.

"I should let you unpack," he backed away.

"I appreciate the help with my grocery bags," she called out to him.

"Anytime. See you around."

"Yes, around," she added, as he backed through the open doorway of the kitchen and made his way through the cottage.

"You do know that TV doesn't work, right?" she heard him holler as she hurried to peek through the kitchen doorway.

She laughed as she saw him standing near her suitcase and he had his hands in his jacket pockets. "I assumed it didn't, and honestly I don't really need it. It's not my thing." He wondered what was her thing. She probably had a Kindle packed to download and read a dozen books. Or maybe she was a writer. He already knew she was a deep thinker. He had witnessed that on the beach earlier today.

"Okay, if you change your mind…you'll need to buy a new one," he laughed out loud and she joined him.

"Gee thanks, Mr. Fix-it."

"Hey now, be nice," he had taken a hand out of his jacket pocket and playfully pointed his finger at her.

"Nice is my middle name." She was teasing but she had thought, *yes, but look where being nice had gotten her.* Maybe if she had not been the nice, compliant, easy-to-please wife, maybe then her husband would not have sought out a bad girl.

"Have a good evening, Poppy Nice…" he closed the door softly behind him and she giggled alone in the cottage.

⨍ ⨍ ⨍

After she unpacked the groceries, Poppy made herself a jalapeño and cheese egg omelet. She finished the bottle of wine with it that she had opened when she arrived. After she left the kitchen, she had unpacking to do. She kicked off her flip flops as she wheeled her suitcase behind her down the hallway, to the second room on the right. The first room had always been her grandparent's room or her parent's, depending who was staying there at the same time. Poppy was a grown woman, but still she could not see herself sleeping in the room that once was theirs. And besides, she wanted to see the bedroom that she and Bobby were forced to share as children. There had been two twin beds and they both complained about sharing their space. Even though deep down neither one of them had thought it was really that awful. Poppy would have given anything now to lie awake, looking up at the ceiling while she and her brother whispered in the dark from bed to bed.

They shared secrets often. In fact, one week before Bobby died, Poppy confessed in their dark bedroom — so he could not see her cheeks flush — that she had experienced her first kiss. *Gross*, her eleven-year-old brother had said aloud. And then, after a pause, he added, *you're still going to be into guy things with me, right? Like baseball and fishing?* Poppy promised him nothing between them had changed.

She abandoned her suitcase in the hallway as she turned the knob of the closed bedroom door. The door creaked on its hinges. She paused before she flipped on the light switch. And when the room was lit, she brought her hand to her mouth. Those twin beds, paralleled in the middle of that room, were still there. The bedding was obviously different. Both had white duvets, bed skirts, and throw pillows. Someone who had been there through the years preferred classy, but simple. Poppy could still visualize her grandmother's hand-made quilts, once covering those beds — *every time, and the last time she was at the cottage.* Poppy was just a girl then, a pre-teen. And now she was a woman in the second act of her life. Bobby's quilt was royal blue with a catcher's mitt sewn on the center. Poppy's was yellow with a pink rose sewn in the middle. Poppy was sure those faded, time-worn quilts were tucked away somewhere still. *Maybe in that very cottage?* She would look. But right now, all she wanted to do was to go sit over there, on those beds. One and then the other. She would position herself on the end of hers and focus her eyes over and onto Bobby's empty twin bed. If she sat still enough, listened closely, focused her eyes just right, he would be there again.

She felt solemn when she sat down on the edge of her bed. And then moments later, she got up and walked a few feet over to his. She ran her open hand overtop the white duvet, she envisioned it to be the blue quilt with the catcher's mitt positioned precisely in the middle. The brown threading, even back then, was loose and frayed.

"I imagine you weren't the last person to sleep in this bed. Not after all these years. But look at it, Bobby. The frame is still the same. The brass headboard probably still rattles with any movement. It's just as you left it. You left much too soon, little brother. I wasn't allowed to talk about you..." Poppy felt the tears spill from her eyes and roll down both of her cheeks. "I missed you. I still do. Being here...it's difficult. It's like I'm forced to feel all of it again. Is this healing? Is this peace?"

There was no answer in that tiny, old bedroom with white-paneled walls and hardwood flooring. "I'm here to find something, Bobby. I don't know what that is, but if you can wrap your arms around my shoulders or pull me by the hand toward it, please do. I'm alone now. And… I'm lost." Poppy ultimately sat down on the bed where the quilt, custom-made for the little boy in the red baseball cap, used to be.

Chapter four

The sun was peering through the closed window blinds when Poppy opened her eyes. She had fallen asleep on the bed that once was Bobby's. She never pulled back the duvet or a sheet to cover her body, still fully clothed in her flared jeans and light-weight black sweater. It could have been the fact that she had a little too much wine, or maybe she had cried herself to sleep last night. Either way, Poppy had not slept that unbelievably well in what felt like forever. Her nights by herself at the townhouse, still in the bed she shared with her husband of twenty-eight years, were endless and lonely. She never slept much anymore. At the cottage, however, Poppy woke up and welcomed the feeling of being rested and energized. She made her way into the living room. The sun was peering through those open window blinds, as Poppy realized she had not tightly closed them the night before — nor had she locked the door. *The cottage on the beach was still a safe place.* Odd to know the one place Poppy had felt especially safe all throughout her childhood was the very same place that destroyed the security of their family. Without Bobby they weren't a family.

Poppy found her suitcase, still where she parked it in the hallway last night. She rolled it down to the first bedroom. She opened the door to the room she remembered either her mother sleeping in alone, or else her grandparents had occupied it. Poppy recalled very few memories of her father being at the cottage. This was a larger bedroom. It had a queen-sized bed with burgundy bedding, again with an all-matching duvet, bed-skirt, and decorative throw pillows. This room also had white paneled walls. That was a staple all throughout the cottage, except for the mint green living room walls. That was still taking some getting used to for Poppy.

She opened her suitcase and found her fluffy white terrycloth robe folded in half on the top. That comfortable, old robe was as aged as the sand on the beach. Well, not really, but Poppy had worn it for decades. She dropped all of her clothes at her feet. Black laced panties, black bra. All of it came off. And like a teenage girl, she piled the clothing at her feet on the floor and left the room, carrying her robe over her forearm. There was no one there that she had to tidy up for. If she wanted to leave her clothes and belongings on the floor or scattered throughout the cottage, she could.

In the bathroom, Poppy flipped on the light and threw back the ruffled, teal, shower curtain. It made a screeching sound from the metal hooks sliding on the metal rod. She turned on the hot water in the bathtub shower. She looked at herself in the mirror. Naked. Yesterday's makeup stained her face. Her hair was matted from sleeping. She looked away, and then she looked back. *What woman at fifty-three years old was completely satisfied with her body?* There were too many changes to dwell on, and more to come. Even still, Poppy was a beautiful woman who had taught her two grown daughters to love themselves, appreciate their bodies, and grasp the changes from year to year because *you're living.* If you have laugh lines, you've enjoyed yourself, you've felt joy. If you have crow's feet, you've squinted while feeling the warmth of the sun on your face. *Live, Laugh, and Love,* she used to say to her girls. And Poppy believed she had parented both CeCe and Tealy by example. *Live.* Poppy most certainly lived. Even after losing her brother and suffocating as a broken family of three with her parents, Poppy had found reasons to go on. This was *her life,* and she knew her little brother would have wanted her to seize it. *Laugh.* Poppy's giggle was contagious, Reed used to tell her that. She missed many things about her husband, but most of all it was the way they were able to laugh together, at each other, and at themselves. Who was laughing now? Poppy had been made a fool of. *Love.* Poppy was a passionate person. She believed in fairytales and happily ever after. Just no longer for herself. She had her day.

≠ ≠ ≠

Her brown hair was blow dried and fell loose above her shoulders. She applied some mascara and lipstick. Just because. She chose a pair of black leggings and a chunky high-low heather gray turtle neck sweater. She wanted to take a morning walk along the beach. This time she left behind her flip flops, which always were too heavy to lift under her feet in the sand.

Poppy crossed her arms over her chest as the chilly air met her every step on the beach. A warm sweater, snug bottoms, and the freedom of bare feet in the sand felt wonderful to her.

The sound of the ocean waves brought Poppy back too quickly to that awful day. There was no saving him, she knew that. But she always wished she could have done more. Her mother, in the midst of shock, panic, and anger, had accused Poppy of *just standing there and letting her brother die.* That was just another thing Poppy was able to rise above in her life.

Poppy walked on. Her stomach growled. She had not eaten or even taken a sip of anything this morning. This walk was first and foremost on her mind. After a few miles down the beach, she eventually turned around to go back. Her thoughts never stopped out there. She thought of Tealy and her grandchildren. Poppy had upset her youngest daughter when she told her of this move. *Temporary or permanent?* She had not been able to give her daughter an answer. *What about help from time to time with the kids, especially the baby, when I have to be somewhere?* Poppy apologized, and then admitted she adored her three grandchildren — but she wanted to enjoy them, not parent them. Poppy did not want her children and grandchildren to consume her, and become her only reason. She still sought her own life, especially now that she was a divorcee. *Maybe she would tire of the beach, tire of this vacation, this escape, and return to Boston to resume her only role of just being a Grandma? Maybe not.*

CeCe was another story. Her life was behind the camera. She worked long hours, she traveled for video shoots. She lived for her career. Or so Poppy had believed. She wondered, and she used to express this to Reed, if there was someone special in her oldest daughter's life who filled her heart with the kind of joy no career can offer. CeCe preferred to keep her life private. She was smart and perceptive. She may have been the only family member who understood that the cottage on Martha's Vineyard was a place Poppy needed to return to.

Poppy's legs felt weak and she was borderline light-headed once she reached the cottage. It was her own fault. She needed nourishment before taking a long walk like that. Poppy was about to step up, onto the boardwalk leading up to the porch, when she looked out toward the water and saw the fishing dock was occupied again. *Had he been out there earlier too when she left to walk the beach?* That red cap. *Would she ever get used to seeing one?* She hadn't yet, and it had been decades. Poppy had long since come to the conclusion that there were a lot of red baseball caps perched on top of heads out there. To cope, she used to tell herself that it was a sign. Whenever she saw one, it was Bobby stopping by to say hello to her. Poppy had never told anyone that. Not even her mother. She wasn't entirely sure if her mother realized that Bobby had been wearing a red baseball cap the day they were all supposed to leave the cottage at the summer's end. They never spoke of it.

"Hiya Dudley," she spoke happily as she stepped onto the dock. She trusted her bare feet wouldn't snag a splinter. His back was to her. His fishing gear, both the tackle box and pole, remained untouched at his side. He turned to her. He didn't appear startled by her presence. His expression was blank. Poppy immediately felt uncomfortable. They hardly knew each other. She really shouldn't have interrupted him — alone in his thoughts — just now.

"Good morning, Poppy," he said, but there was nothing good in the sound of his voice. It was as if he was spent and could barely speak a word without making a serious effort. Like having a sore throat, the words faded as he spoke and were almost inaudible. Poppy wondered if he was under the weather. If so, why was he there? She watched him stare out at the ocean.

"The ocean is a good listener," she offered.

"Excuse me?" he said, his voice sounding stronger this time, as he looked up at her, but she couldn't see his eyes under the bill of his red cap.

"We send out all of our deepest thoughts when we're walking along in the sand or staring out at the water. I guess if we waited long enough, listened intently enough, we'd get a response. The answer is in the wind or the waves." Poppy believed that now. She knew she always had a desire to return there one day. The peace she yearned for had to be out there. In the water. The waves. The white sanded beach. Poppy had not found it anywhere else in her life thus far. She was counting on this return to the cottage to be what she sought. If anything, she wanted closure.

"I can't seem to find that connection. I need more, I suppose. Maybe fishing is what's therapeutic for me," Dudley admitted.

Then why had he just been sitting on the dock – right now and yesterday when she first arrived on the island – with his fishing gear within reach, but not in use? "What are you waiting for then?" Poppy asked, wondering if maybe the conditions were not good, or possibly Dudley preferred being in a boat.

"Every single day, for months on end, for an hour or so, I've been right here, in this exact spot, with my gear. My wife insisted that I come. She thought I was doing something for me, keeping my sanity that way. You know, like you implied, she sees the ocean as being some sort of a shrink." Poppy listened raptly. She tried to imagine what his wife might look like. She wondered if she would meet her. Poppy was designed that way.

She was into meanings — who belonged with whom, and why the universe had aligned certain people and time and circumstance brought them together. She believed with all of her heart that she was meant to meet Reed the moment she was a college graduate. They made a life, a family together. It was the time, the day, the moment when another woman waltzed into his life and robbed a part of him that Poppy now cursed. She couldn't fathom why. To hell with destiny, and time and circumstance. That woman stole her husband. And Reed clearly had not resisted all too strongly either.

"I understand if you want to be alone," Poppy began. "I came here, to the island, and specifically to this cottage, to get lost for awhile...and then maybe find my way." Poppy realized she had not made much sense to someone who didn't know her story. But the notion was comprehendible to her.

"Alone," Dudley repeated. "I hate that word, and even more so I cannot stand the thought of feeling it." *For the rest of his life.* He looked down at his bare feet on the dock.

Poppy was careful to respond to what he admitted. She made her way down, to a sitting position right beside him. She crisscrossed her legs in her black tights. And then he finally looked at her from underneath the bill of his cap. She saw tears welling up in his hazel eyes. He sniffed, trying to keep his nose from running. "I hate it, too. More than you know," Poppy told him, referring to being alone. "Listen, I don't want to pry. I don't mean to be bossy or all-knowing. I'm just going to speak from my heart. I know pain. I know sorrow. Sometimes we cannot avoid either. It smacks us in the face and pretty much says, *here ya go, deal!* If you're able to fix what's going on in your life, you may want to make that effort, give it a try." Poppy caught herself. It was in her hands to mend what went wrong with her life, specifically with her marriage, but she chose not to. Was she being a hypocrite by telling Dudley to try to save his marriage? What if his wife had been unfaithful like Reed? That was a pain most people just could not forgive and forget. She felt as if she overstepped. Especially because she did not know Dudley's story.

"It's out of my hands," Dudley told her, and Poppy nodded. She understood.

They sat amid shared silence for awhile. Listening to the waves, splashing up underneath the dock. Not speaking wasn't awkward, but Poppy did feel as if she had intruded on his time. He said he didn't like the idea of being alone, and yet it appeared as if he didn't want to share his story on that dock in the ocean right now. Just as Poppy was searching her brain for an excuse, a reason to get up and go, Dudley spoke again.

"My wife lost a very brave, but brutal battle to multiple sclerosis today," Dudley spoke those words softly, and Poppy felt overwhelmed with the compassion that had just risen in her chest. *Death.* He was talking about the kind of loss that stabbed at the very core of a human being. Whether it was shocking and sudden, or forthcoming and complete with unsettled goodbyes — death was the absolute worst kind of loss. Poppy was certain of it. Losing Bobby had nearly killed her. Parting ways, severing her life with Reed had damaged her, but somewhere beyond that pain and heartbreak Poppy knew eventually she would survive. And besides, Reed was still around to be angry with. Her precious little innocent brother had been dead for forty-one years. "Oh no...I am sorry." She didn't have the slightest idea. Of course she didn't. *They had just met, why would he have confided in her about something so painful and personal?* He had now.

"We knew the end was close, but to actually be prepared when the moment arrives and it really does happen is unfathomable. This pain and emptiness is bottomless." As Dudley spoke with complete sincerity, Poppy reached out and touched his hand. He never pulled away, so she held it while she spoke.

"Bottomless. Yes. Grief is never ending. Time will pull you through in its own way and at its own pace. Just know that it's going to suck the life out of you for a long damn time." Poppy gently squeezed his hand before she pulled hers away from his. Sitting close may have been enough. There wasn't much personal space between them right now. Touching suddenly felt intrusive, and because she had been the one to initiate it, she also ceased it.

"Tell me your story, Poppy." He had recognized the sadness in her eyes. "I don't want to feel this alone."

She wasn't ready. Sharing the pain of losing her little brother to the death grip of the sea, while she sat on a stable dock right above those murderous waves, now decades later, felt wrong. She wouldn't use Bobby's memory like that. She didn't want anyone's pity. She wouldn't be forced to admit that all these years later she still felt like a victim struck down by death and shoved into the quicksand of grief. She had come there to heal. If reliving that pain had to happen, she was adamant about doing it on her own terms. She very much sympathized with this man. But she only wanted to offer him some comfort. She wasn't here to bond over grief. Hers was decades old. His was brand new. *Was that even a comparison?*

"I have to go," Poppy stood up abruptly, and Dudley was taken aback and startled. He also quickly made it to his feet. He had overstepped. *Was he sorry? Had he wanted something bad to have happened to this woman in order to feel less pity for himself?* Of course not. He was just looking for someone who could relate — and understand the rawness of his pain right now. And Poppy had been the one to reach out first. "I'm sorry. I can't give you what you need. I don't have it in me to revisit that kind of pain," Poppy admitted. *She was there though, wasn't she?* That was the first step, or more like the first hurdle. She had arrived on island and entered the cottage. And, thus far, she survived the return.

Dudley was silent. Poppy was partially embarrassed and partially angry. Angry at herself —because she thought she was ready for this.

She turned to walk away. It was what she had done before on that very beach. She followed her mother's lead. Leave and never look back. Poppy was not her mother's daughter though. She had overcome so much more. She had returned to Martha's Vineyard to delve deep and that was going to require looking back. Dudley wasn't the answer though. It made no sense for him to be a part of this equation. How could Poppy drag him through the pain and confusion she had never truly faced head on? She couldn't. Not when he was brand new to the suffocating feeling of grief.

She couldn't look at him anymore. Just as she made a hurried attempt to escape him, the wind picked up. The gust was unexpected, fierce, and strong. It nearly threw her off balance. It was enough to prevent Poppy from stepping away.

And it was also enough to take the hat right off of Dudley's head. "Shit!" she heard him say, just as she watched it fly in the air above their heads. The wind took it then, swirled it, and it landed on the very edge of that fishing dock. The wind instantly calmed and Poppy ran, in an attempt to save the cap. She fell to her knees to stop herself from falling off that edge. The red baseball cap was safe in her hands. She clenched it so hard with both hands that her knuckles instantly turned white.

She looked up at Dudley. His hair was curly and matted where the cap had fit snugly on his head. His bare feet were close to her knees on that dock's edge, and her knees hurt from the brunt fall to them. He wanted to say *it's just a hat.* But the intensity of her actions just now had stopped him from speaking anything but "Thank you," as he bent down to reach for his cap. Poppy wouldn't let go. In fact, she was trembling. Not just her hands that gripped the red baseball cap, but her entire body shook.

Dudley made his way slowly down to the dock beside her. "It's okay," he heard himself say. He reached for his cap again, and this time she began to loosen her grip on it.

"You must think I'm crazy," she spoke, and Dudley shook his head no, but really he just had that exact thought. "Four decades ago, a red baseball cap was sucked under the relentless waves out here. And my little brother was wearing it."

Chapter five

Tealy Stewart counted seven rings before the call to her sister, CeCe Brennan went to voicemail. It was naptime for her baby boy, and her girls were in school, prekindergarten and kindergarten. This was a rare free minute for her, and Tealy deemed this phone call as important. *Damn her sister for not being available.*

Their mother running away to the cottage was wrong. Tealy and her father agreed on that. And now Tealy wanted her big sister's thoughts. She had a feeling the free-spirit in her would cheer on their mother to enjoy the independence of being a runaway. CeCe hadn't even been close to being as hurt and irate as Tealy when the truth surfaced about their father having another family. *So we have a half brother? I'd like to meet him.* Cece's attitude had actually, eventually, softened Tealy a bit. She initially wanted to hate her father forever. Instead, they were on speaking terms. Still, Tealy had sided with her mother. CeCe never took sides. She just rallied for herself.

Call me when you get this message. I don't like this whole thing with mom being on Martha's Vineyard for infinity. I mean it C. Call me.

Tealy ended the call and threw her phone on the sofa cushion before she plopped down beside it. Her husband was out of town on a business trip. She was juggling three children all by herself. Not that she wasn't used to being at the helm of their family and managing everything except for earning money for their livelihood. She was just missing Grant for obvious reasons, and he was another adult under their roof to talk to. And that was also partly why she was miffed at her mother for leaving. She felt abandoned. This stay-at-home mom thing —her dream no less— had put her in a slump. And Tealy needed help being pulled out of it. She ran her hands through her cropped dark hair, leaned her head back against the sofa, and closed her eyes. *May as well rest while the baby naps.*

⁄ ⁄ ⁄

CeCe Brennan was behind the camera, the place where she felt most comfortable in any setting, whether it was for work or for play. Today was an exception though. Her three-inch heeled bone-colored, suede booties were rubbing the tender skin raw on the back of her heels. She rarely wore heels. She was five-nine and didn't feel the need to tower over people any higher than she already had. Her matching off-the-shoulder dress felt shorter than it had when she slipped it on in her bedroom this morning. CeCe wasn't comfortable. The sun was shining and the cool sixty-five degree air temperature should have made for a beautiful day at the park. But this day didn't feel beautiful. CeCe stepped out from behind the camera and made her way up to the makeshift altar in the park. Her dark hair, styled in loose curls down past her shoulders, felt tousled by the sudden wind. The female minister was in the middle of her dearly beloved speech to the bride and groom when CeCe resumed her position, her role as maid of honor. The small, intimate fall wedding in Boston's city park was going to be a day to remember, CeCe's best friend Jen had stated when she asked her to document the wedding ceremony and then stand by her side while she married the love of her life. CeCe reluctantly agreed.

She stood beside her best friend and looked overtop her head at the groom. Stu Brentwood had jet black hair and piercing blue eyes. He was two inches taller than CeCe, and he towered his bride at five-four. Because Jen was short (even in stilettos), CeCe imagined Stu to be pledging his love for her. *His eyes were focused on her now.*

There were people watching, she reminded herself to keep it together. Those rows of white folding chairs in the park were occupied by her best friend's family, the groom's family, and many friends that they shared alike. *Keep your cool, C. Remember your poker face.*

CeCe was never going to settle down. She was thirty-one years old and marriage wasn't for her. That was what she had told Stu. At first, he wasn't looking to make an honest woman out of her. They were only having fun. Their secret affair had been ongoing for three years, which was longer than CeCe's best friend, the bride today in the park, had dated and been engaged to the groom. The fact was, Stu had asked CeCe to marry him first. He wanted to break off his relationship with her best friend, and go public with her. He wanted CeCe to be his wife. That was the very same time frame that her father's shocking secret had surfaced in Boston. CeCe was just like him. The apple had not fallen very far from that damn tree. She, too, was a cheat and a liar. All for sex —and love. It was love for CeCe. She just never would admit it. And the absolute worst part of it all was CeCe, nor the groom in the park today, had ended the relationship. CeCe was going to be an official cheat once this ceremony concluded. Married or not, she wouldn't give up this man. *Her father would understand if he knew. And her mother would kill her— if she knew.*

CeCe looked down at her feet in those uncomfortable booties as she stepped away from the passionately kissing bride and groom. She acted as if the camera needed her attention. The last thing, however, that CeCe wanted to do was press her eye to the lens and zoom-in on the lip lock between her best friend and her lover. That's why she had looked down and continued to step away from the happy couple as the crowd that gathered for the afternoon wedding in the park clapped and cheered.

✎ ✎ ✎

Poppy left the window blinds open well after sunset. She stood in front of the middle window now, her arms folded across her chest. She thought back to being on that fishing dock, the one she couldn't see out there in the darkness now. Dudley was in pain. The pain of loss. His wife just died. It was still the same day, her death date.

"I'm sorry," Dudley had said to her when she was on her knees, at the edge of the fishing dock, with his red cap in her hands. It made sense to him then. The sadness he saw in her

45

eyes at that cottage, at that beach — stemmed from the loss of her brother.

I'm sorry. That was all he had said before he gently took his red cap from her hands and walked off the dock. His grief was raw. Poppy had not expected anything more from him. *Or had she?* She certainly never got it, as Dudley just walked away.

There were two outside lights mounted on each end of the wraparound porch. The illumination on the boardwalk was just enough for Poppy to see a figure out there. Walking. She felt like she should be startled, but she wasn't. The silhouette that she was able to distinguish in a split second was familiar to her. She stepped toward her unlocked door and swung it open before he could knock.

"Oh, hey, you saw me coming? I debated on this… it's late, it's dark…" Poppy smiled sincerely. Dudley was wearing faded, baggy jeans, a long-sleeved black t-shirt, and this time a black baseball cap. She wondered if that was purposeful. *Would he not wear that red cap — the only cap she had seen him wear until now — around her anymore?*

"It is late, but I've never been afraid of the dark," Poppy stepped back. "Come on in."

She waited a moment. *Would she ask him to sit down? If he wanted a glass of wine?* He never gave her a chance to, as he spoke first.

"The reason I'm here is… I just want to explain what happened earlier," Dudley paused. Poppy stood directly in front of him near the door he had just closed. She was barefoot. He was wearing flip flops. She still had on her black leggings and heather gray turtleneck sweater.

"It's fine, really," Poppy stated, trying to ease Dudley's worry. So what if he left her on the fishing dock when she had been trembling after she admitted her brother had died in that water below them. Many years ago. He didn't owe her anything. She surely wouldn't fire him as the cottage caretaker, if that's what he was concerned about.

"I was rude," Dudley stated. "I should have stayed... and listened if you wanted to talk about it. What happened to your brother must have been awful. So tragic. I was only thinking of my own pain, but that was insensitive."

"This isn't necessary," Poppy waved her hand in the air. "You have enough going on right now." *There was no need for him to worry about her feelings.*

"That's just it. I don't," Dudley replied. "My wife, she preplanned everything. She'd been sick for awhile. She didn't want me to have to deal with anything after she was... gone. She chose cremation. She asked that our sons and myself scatter her ashes wherever we choose and whenever we are ready. We know she wants to be near the ocean," Dudley paused, and he looked down at the floor. "My sons, they are twins, and they both attend Boston University. They were here all week, at their mother's bedside when she took her last breath. And now they've resumed their lives at school. No memorial service will take place. Neither one of us have surviving parents. It is what it is. Sharon died. My boys left. Friends and some family called, some will stop by, I guess, or send a sympathy card if people even still do that anymore. Life resumes now."

47

Poppy felt sad for him. Just listening to him speak was as if he was expected to carry on with life without a second thought, without batting an eye. Grief didn't work that way, Poppy knew all too well. She had witnessed her parents try to shove grief under the rug. "Dudley, do you have time to come sit down? Would you like a glass of wine?"

He nodded his head, and followed her into the kitchen. Without further invitation, Dudley pulled out a chair from underneath the small, round kitchen table, and he sat down while Poppy poured the white wine into stemless glasses on the countertop.

When she joined him at the table, she immediately took a long sip before she spoke what was on her mind. "I don't know much about you and your family," she began, "and I realize you know very little about me. I told you that I lost my brother. I've accepted the fact that he's gone, but I've never dealt with the pain, if that makes any sense at all. That's why I'm here. I'm at a crossroad in my life. I need to be here now more than ever."

"Are you alone?" Dudley asked her outright. He had no idea, and he wanted to know more about her.

"I have two grown daughters, one is married with three small children, and the other is single and loving it," Poppy smiled. "And I'm recently divorced." He never expected more, but she explained further. "We had twenty-eight wonderful years, but come to find out I'm pretty damn clueless, oblivious to secrets and lies." Dudley frowned. Poppy continued. "My ex-husband's an oral surgeon. I was a stay-at-home mom to our girls. We had a very cozy life, but one family wasn't quite enough for him. Three months ago, I caught him visibly upset while reading an obituary in the newspaper. He wrote off his emotions as nothing. I followed him when he left the house the next day. He went to a funeral wake for a woman who had been his mistress for two decades. I saw a young man there, barely twenty years old, who was a carbon copy of my ex-husband when I first met him thirty years ago. Reed had a mistress and a son, a family on the side of having a life, a marriage and a family with me!" Retelling the story still upset her. She took another long swallow of wine. Dudley watched her closely.

"Jesus Christ. I could barely handle one family," he stated, with a look of shock on his face that had not subsided.

Poppy laughed. "Yeah, most of us realize one is enough. Reed always did think he was superhuman. The sad part was, so did I."

"I'm sorry that happened," Dudley offered. "It just seems so far-fetched to be true. I mean, to be going on for that long?"

"Exactly, but unfortunately it's my life. Or, it was my life. Now, I begin again. Here."

"So, you really are staying for the long haul?" Dudley asked her.

Poppy nodded. "I have no plan to go back to Boston anytime soon."

"I know what it's like not to have a plan," Dudley offered.

"Your life will come together how it's supposed to. Just give it time. I think that's the one thing I learned after I lost my brother. The things that happened in my life were going to fall into place whether I kicked and screamed, or just patiently coasted while it all worked out. I was meant to meet Reed, meant to be a mother to our girls. I was always sure of that. But, now this? Now I am faced with life alone at fifty-three years old because my husband lied and cheated. I'm starting over, not because I'm strong enough to—but because I owe it to myself."

Those were powerful words, and in a way Dudley was inspired. But there also was a part of him that felt confused and angry. He didn't want the second act of his life to be spent without his wife. *What good was life alone?* He thought of Poppy as brave for doing what she was doing, but he wasn't about to sit back and coast alone for this ride. Dudley knew what he wanted now. And she was right in front of him.

Chapter six

They talked for hours. It was well after midnight when Poppy yawned behind the rim of her wine glass. Of the three bottles she just picked up at the market, there was only one left. They weren't drunk, but they were tipsy and incredibly relaxed as they sat at the kitchen table. Dudley had pushed his chair back, and stretched his legs straight out in front of him, crossing at his ankles where his denim ended and his bare feet began.

"I saw that," Dudley stated. "It's past your bedtime, and we don't need to open another bottle of wine. I should go."

Aside from the yawn she just now failed to suppress, Poppy felt like she could sit there and talk to him all night long. They shared stories of each other's pasts. The people in their lives. The people gone from their lives, some too soon. *Poppy's brother. Dudley's wife.* They bonded tonight, and Poppy wondered if he felt it, too. The pull. The draw. The connection. The answer to uncertainty and loneliness was companionship. This was new to her. Poppy didn't just go around making new friends. She barely had any old friends. No one consistently stuck around for her. Her family was her constant. She considered her husband, year after year, to be the closest person she had to a best friend. Again, when she let go of him, Poppy lost so much more than her marriage.

"This was nice," Poppy told him, following his lead to bring the night to a close. "Thank you for real conversation and a good listening ear."

"Right back at you, Poppy," Dudley stated with a smile. His eyes were still pained, but he looked content right now. He twisted his black cap around earlier and the bill was still backwards, near the base of his neck. Despite the signs of aging on his face, he looked youthful and boyish to her. She watched him stand, and when she followed him to her feet, her head instantly felt light. "You okay?" Dudley reached for her upper arm, but she remained steady without his help.

"Yeah, me and my low tolerance," Poppy giggled. *Giggled? Really, when was the last time she had genuinely laughed?*

"Well it's a good thing you're not the one driving home," he stated, with a wink.

Poppy's eyes widened. "Yes, but should you be?" This was new to her as well. Reed was always in control. She could count the times on one hand when he was actually drunk. They were young then, and carefree, and that was the era before they were married with responsibilities. Reed could handle alcohol. He never drank beer after beer. He sometimes shared a bottle of wine with her. Most of the time, he indulged in a glass of scotch.

"I assure you, I'll be fine." He appeared confident, and not the least bit drunk. Poppy wondered if he nursed one or two glasses of wine all night while she sucked both bottles dry. She hadn't really paid attention.

They walked through the kitchen, into the living room, and to his exit. The front door. This was her second night on island and Dudley had been there, at the cottage, for both. She wondered if his presence ceased for a day or two, would she be lonely there? She hadn't the chance to know. Yet.

He turned to her before reaching for the door handle. "You made what began as a very sad day for me, not so awful. The world is still turning. Life will go on. You've helped me to see that."

Poppy smiled softly at him. "I know a little bit about how you feel. You've helped me too, possibly with something I didn't even know I needed the presence of in my life. A friend."

Dudley opened his arms to her, and Poppy stepped forward and into an embrace that instantly felt like familiar. Like home. As if she was meant to fit there. The feeling left her taken aback and comfortable at the very same time. *Had she ever felt that way before?* If she had, she failed to recall when or how.

As they slowly released their grip from each other, their faces slightly touched. Her cheek brushed his. She felt the prickle of the whiskers on his unshaven face. Her body instantly heated. Her first instinct was to pull away. Back up. Stop this feeling. But her brain and body were not in agreement.

Poppy turned her head just as Dudley moved his. Before they realized, or maybe they had, their lips were close. Poppy could smell the wine on his breath. His lips were parted. She realized hers were too. He leaned in a little. And she did too. His full lips were warm and soft as he met hers with them. She felt her arms rise and reach behind the base of his neck where the bill of his cap ended. His arms were around her, his hands on the small of her back. On her bare skin as her sweater had lifted when she reached her arms around him. He was only, at best, two inches taller than her. Their kiss deepened. Poppy couldn't think. She didn't want to. She only wanted to feel and to keep feeling. Just like this.

They made out like teenagers. And then the touching began. It was as if they both already needed more. Again, Poppy didn't think. This didn't need to be analyzed or rationed. Deep down, she knew that would come later. She felt his hand move up her sweater. He found her breasts and grazed a nipple through her bra. Her desire for this, for him, intensified. She never stopped him when he lifted her sweater and moved it up, over her head, and off of her body. He kissed the spill of her breasts, lifting out of her lacy bra cups. She reached behind her own back and undid the clasp to set herself free for him. He looked, he touched her gently with his fingertips, and then his lips and his tongue devoured her. She arched her back and he supported her all the way down to the floor near the sofa. She helped him out of his shirt. It joined his cap already on the floor. He was bare-chested and barefoot in jeans. She was bare-chested and barefoot in tights. Their limbs were entangled. Their lips were exploring. Dudley found her core with his fingers through her leggings. She reacted with a moan that further aroused him. He stretched and moved the tights down to reveal her. She was pantyless. He groaned and made his way down her body to her open legs. She wanted this more than she ever had. She was free to feel, to do anything. She felt young again as this man made her orgasm at the will of his tongue. She cried out just as he pulled himself up onto his knees. He met her hands with his own at his zipper, covering his fly. She was eager. And when she freed him, he kicked off his denim and straddled her on his knees. He too couldn't think of anything else. But he would later. He closed his eyes when she took him into her hands. She rolled her thumb over the tip of his manhood and he felt eighteen again. He could not hold out much longer. His body was starved for this. He couldn't remember the last time with his wife. Before she became too frail. He had resorted to stroking himself in the shower. This was a million and one times better. He wanted this so badly he could have cried. He pulled out of her hands and slipped between her legs. At first, he was gentle in his effort to feel her with his entire length. Her body welcomed him, her response sent him reeling. He thrusted hard and swiftly. She wrapped her legs around his lower back. He was strong and confident in how he was pleasing her. She moaned, repeatedly. The sights and sounds of sex sent them both into ecstasy. And with his release, he pulled out of her, and they lay side by side, naked, on their backs. Staring up at the ceiling. They were no longer touching the moment their minds began to reel, in an attempt to make sense of this. They shared the same thought. *What had they done?* Sex between strangers. Right or wrong? Ridiculously soon for a man who just lost his wife? Too much for a woman who was still in love with her ex-husband? Sex. That's all this was.

Chapter seven

Getting dressed in front of each other was awkward and purposely rushed. They spoke very little, and made fleeting eye contact.

"Good thing we were on the floor, your blinds are still open." *Nervous laughs.*

Standing there in her leggings and turtleneck sweater, sans a bra, Poppy found the courage to speak as Dudley grabbed the last of his clothing and prepared to leave her cottage. "This is not the norm for me..." She wanted to be clear. She was not *that kind of a woman.* "I could blame the wine, but I do believe it was my loneliness and your pending fear of it that led us to just stop thinking."

Dudley looked at her. He agreed, for the most part. He was afraid of what the future held for him. He feared emptiness, and never being with a woman again. He wanted more than just sex though. He wasn't sure where to go from here with Poppy, but he was certain this wasn't the last time they would be together in the full sense. "You're a beautiful woman, Poppy."

"Thank you," she said in almost a whisper. She felt self-conscious. This man saw her naked and did things to her body that she already wanted to feel again, and one compliment had made her feel uncomfortable.

He closed the door quickly behind him.

✂ ✂ ✂

Poppy was asleep on the white suede sofa in the living room. The sun lit up the entire room on the other side of her closed eyelids. She sensed daylight in her sleep. She also believed she was in the middle of a dream when she heard her girls giggling. There was a ruckus on the front porch. A thud. Some roaring laughter. This, Poppy was certain, was a sweet dream of her daughters, getting along as they sometimes did. When the door of her cottage flew open and Poppy was jolted from a not-so-deep sleep, she realized it was no dream. Her girls were on island.

Poppy's first thought, as both CeCe and Tealy turned their heads and made eye contact with their mother on the sofa, was *Jesus Christ, what if Dudley had spent the night?*

"Girls!" Poppy was on her feet as she spoke, and then she realized how hung over she felt. Her mouth was dry, her throat felt as if she was trying to swallow cotton. The room spun a little. The sun was too damn bright already. She tried to retain her composure in front of CeCe and Tealy. "What are you two doing here?"

"If you checked your messages, you would know," Tealy scolded her, while CeCe shrugged without comment. She was the one who thought it was a bad idea to interrupt their mother's alone time. She had asked for it, and yet just a few days later Tealy had convinced CeCe to arrive on island to *check on mom, and have a serious, sit down conversation with her about what she's doing at the family cottage* — after never being back since their Uncle Bobby drowned. It was strange to think of having an uncle because he was just an eleven-year-old boy when his life ended. The fact was CeCe wasn't there to delve deep into their mother's thoughts. She only wanted to appease her sister, and especially escape her messed up life in Boston. Maybe here, she could find a way to block out the upsetting flashes in her mind of her best friend and her lover getting married and going on their honeymoon.

"I'm not going to make excuses for needing some space," Poppy stated, as she ran her fingers through what she assumed was bed head. She, however, had not slept a full-night's sleep. There was Dudley. And then only what felt like a few hours of sleep on the sofa afterward, until sunrise.

"Right, we get you, mom," CeCe finally spoke. "We are only here for a couple of days. Tealy needs peace of mind that you aren't losing your shit here. And then, she has her rug rats to return to, and I have a job." Tealy rolled her eyes. She was five-five, a good four inches shorter than her sister who was three years her senior. Her dark hair was cropped short with full bangs parted to one side, whereas CeCe's dark locks were long and naturally wavy. They both had their mother's hair. Poppy had chosen, in her mature age, to wear hers at shoulder length. The three of them, all with their own unique style, were striking. CeCe was wearing full-length dark-washed flared jeans and a skin tight heather gray cowl neck sweater. She, like her mother, was prepared for the sand with flip flops on her feet. Tealy, however, complained it would be too chilly for bare feet and had worn socks and tennis shoes with cropped black leggings and an oversized pale pink hoodie that she had purchased from her yoga gym.

"I'm not losing anything here. I came here because of what I've already lost," Poppy clarified. "This place, this cottage that I remember so vividly from my childhood, is where I need to be for awhile." Poppy thought of Dudley. She was hardly lost and lonely when he was around. Especially last night. It had been a very long time since a man showed her that kind of affection. Reed included. Poppy had definitely missed the signs in her marriage — from her adulterous husband. She had forgotten the eagerness of love making. She used to believe she was getting too old for passion. How wrong she was.

"See!" CeCe turned to Tealy, and Tealy in response elbowed her in the ribs.

"I'm not really all that prepared for guests here. You two can share a room," Poppy felt a pang deep in her heart. That was the exact same thing her mother used to tell her and Bobby. "And I guess that leaves me with my mother's old room." She let out a sarcastic laugh. There was nothing to hide from her daughters. They knew, all of their lives, how strained that relationship was. Their grandmother was not the most warm and fuzzy woman in their world.

"Have you slept in any room since you arrived?" Tealy asked, and Poppy thought of falling asleep on top of the bedding on Bobby's old twin bed. And then last night...on the sofa after sex on the floor. She could have blushed at the mere thought, but willed herself not to.

"Looks like you're into just leaving your delicates wherever you unclothe yourself," CeCe added, as she bent over and retrieved her mother's lacy black bra on the floor underneath the sofa. This time Poppy did blush.

She swiped her bra from her oldest daughter's hand. "I'll take that, and yes, when I'm alone I do what I want." The girls grinned at each other and Poppy pulled them both into a group hug, bra in hand and all. And then they heard her say, "It's good to have my girls here."

⨭ ⨭ ⨭

It was a place she should have brought them to. Her girls could have grown up visiting and knowing the cottage, and relishing the sand and the sun on that beach. It just wasn't on Poppy's radar. She had followed her mother's lead and believed she couldn't possibly return to a place of tragedy and pain. Once again, her mother was wrong. Poppy realized that now. She wanted to heal there, and so far she felt like that could happen. For the two days ahead, Poppy was going to focus on showing her girls a little part of their family's history and perhaps they would make a few memories of their own.

The girls scrambled eggs and prepared toast while Poppy insisted she needed a morning shower. Her body felt feminine to her again. It was strange to feel that way, but she did. She felt sexy having curves and full breasts. Dudley's body had very few imperfections. He was fifty-five years old. His middle was a little thick, but his quads and rear end were rock hard. His manhood was a lot to handle, compared to the men Poppy had been with in her life, but she was hardly complaining. She recalled those intimate details while she had some alone time as she got ready in the bathroom, and then across the hall in the bedroom that was now hers for a couple days. She slipped into a pair of gray sweatpants and a navy blue Boston University t-shirt, a token of her girls being alumni. Her hair was blow dried and left to fall where it may onto her shoulders. Her feet were bare, and a little sand coated on the bottoms already as she shuffled through the living room and into the kitchen for breakfast.

"I could get used to this," Poppy declared as she made her way to the table and found a hot plate of food awaiting her.

"Well don't, because we have lives, mother," CeCe was quick to point out.

"Of course, but I am touched by your impromptu visit just to check on me. I mean, Tealy you have the kids to tend to…and C, can your job survive a day without you?" Poppy wasn't being snarky to CeCe. She knew her daughter was a successful, important career woman.

CeCe didn't mind if her mother was being sarcastic or not. She gave her a lopsided grinned while she chewed a mouthful of eggs and then bit off a piece of toast as well.

"Grant can handle the kids. It's good for him to go at it alone. I do it twenty-four, seven," Tealy chimed in.

"Sure, and you need a break now and then," Poppy stated, sincerely.

"Exactly! I wish Grant understood that. I mean really, mom! Why can't you spend a week here and then come back to the townhouse? The kids miss you!" Was that plea really for her grandchildren, or was Tealy being entirely selfish? Poppy realized her youngest daughter, spoiled all of her life, was most likely missing out on yoga and the occasional lunch with her girlfriends. Poppy had spent much of her time with her grandchildren prior to escaping to the cottage.

"And I miss them, honey. Tell them that for me. Hugs and kisses until I see my little loves again." Poppy avoided commenting on the length of her plans to stay on island, and while Tealy looked like she was going to pout for awhile, CeCe watched her mother closely. *Something was different about her. What had changed? Had this place already brought her a sense of peace?*

"So, how have you been spending your time here since you arrived?" CeCe asked their mother.

Poppy finished chewing — partly to buy herself some time — before she spoke. "Well this is only day three," Poppy began. "You two must really struggle to function without me when I'm MIA." Poppy was teasing, and her girls simultaneously rolled their eyes at her. "Seriously, what have I accomplished here? I made it through the front door. It took me awhile to soak it all in, and especially to get back to the bedroom that Bobby and I bunked together in as kids. It's hard to be here and it's healing to be here. The beach, the ocean, both threaten to suck the life out of me when I'm out there. It's excruciating to remember standing in that sand, watching my brother go under the water, I don't know, two or three times, and then never surface." Poppy cleared her throat and took a sip of the orange juice on the table in front of her.

"God, that's awful," Tealy spoke first.

CeCe nodded in harmony. "You've never kept that story from us, or hid your emotions. I think Teal and I both feel like we knew Bobby, or at least all there was to know about him from your perspective, in your big sister eyes."

Poppy smiled. "Thank you for saying that, honey. I want that so much. He would have been a fun uncle, and I can only imagine the beautiful children he would have had. But, he wasn't given the chance. It's just so unfair." Poppy stopped talking when she noticed her girls were both teary.

"You've said that Keegan reminds you of him," Tealy stated, referring to her eighteen-month-old son.

"Yes, already, he does. That mop of blond hair and his no-fear approach to the world. How fitting that he's Bobby's namesake, too. Keegan Robert feeds my soul." Poppy sighed as she smiled.

"That no fear approach runs in the family," CeCe chided, referring to herself and the man she inherited that characteristic from — her father, Reed Brennan.

"I'll say," Tealy agreed, "and if you ask me, Dad has way too much of it running through his veins. He ripped our family apart for chrissakes!"

That immediately saddened Poppy. To know that her husband had disappointed his family, his daughters, was terrible. And obviously unforgivable.

"It's old news now, Tealy. Let it go. Mom has. She divorced him. She's moving on with her life." CeCe's words struck Poppy in an odd way. *Was that what she was doing?* Her sudden, unexpected, and completely impromptu deed with Dudley last night certainly was a giant step forward. She wasn't looking to replace a husband. She didn't want to belong to another man again. Being a wife was no longer of interest to her. Having a lover, however, was surprisingly another story. *Would Dudley be back? Would she date other men, maybe someday if or when she returned to Boston?* Time would tell. But, for the first time since she divorced Reed, Poppy was open to seeing what the rest of her life could offer her. She was a fifty-three-year old woman, not eighty-three. There was a lot of living left to do. This return to the cottage had already taught Poppy that.

"I don't understand you. Dad hurt us. He betrayed all of us by having another family, practically all of our lives. And you defend him?" Tealy's accusation was true and it stung. CeCe knew all too well why. She was caught up in a web of betrayal herself. The thrill. The addiction. It was too much to give up. And then there was love. She never chose who she was going to fall in love with. It just happened. She had just, unfortunately, had not known how to commit. She was all about embracing fun. Until someone got hurt. And, right now, CeCe was the one hurting.

"I'm not rehashing this with you again!" There was obvious annoyance in CeCe's voice. Tealy was prepared to press her further, but they were suddenly interrupted.

Two loud knocks and the front door of the cottage was opened. "Special delivery for the beautiful woman of the house," all three of them heard a voice say.

Both CeCe and Tealy creased their brows. They were instantly uncomfortable with a stranger just walking in on them. Their mother needed to make a habit of locking her door. It was Poppy who knew exactly who the voice belonged to. *Dudley.*

She swallowed whole the generous bite of toast she had just put into her mouth. And Poppy was the first one to stand up from the kitchen table just as Dudley was coming through the open doorway of the kitchen. He stopped suddenly in his tracks when he saw that Poppy had company. He had noticed an additional vehicle in the parking lot, but that could have been for any of the cottages along the beach. He knew Poppy was alone. But she wasn't. And he thought quickly on his feet as he saw Poppy's eyes widen when her back was to her daughters.

"The centerpiece you ordered," he said, handing a half a dozen yellow long-stem roses to her in an elaborate crystal vase.

"Ordered… yes, thank you!" Poppy quickly retrieved the arrangement from Dudley as he nodded. She saw a mischievous gleam in his eyes and that actually relaxed her a bit as she spoke. "Girls, this is Dudley Connors, the caretaker of our cottage. Dudley, these are my daughters. They surprised me this morning and will be staying here for the next two days." It was good information for him to know. He would for sure stay away, or at least not be so quick to barge in unannounced. He wasn't sure he should have bought her flowers *the morning after* anyway. That was the reason why ultimately he had chosen yellow roses — and not red.

Both CeCe and Tealy thought it was strange for their mother to utilize the caretaker to run tedious errands. She wasn't like that. She was entirely self-sufficient. Tealy wrote that thought off as *whatever*, but it was CeCe who stared long at her mother once more. There was that aura about her again that CeCe had picked up on earlier. Something was going on at that cottage. And whatever it was, it agreed with Poppy Brennan.

Chapter eight

The air temperature had already warmed to fifty-eight degrees, and the sun was shining so bright through the cottage windows that it was coercing the three of them to walk the beach after breakfast.

Poppy was adamant about getting outside to enjoy the beautiful day. She told her girls it was the best weather yet since she arrived on island. And, for November, those days could be few and far between.

"Few and far between for you, mom, because you are the only one staying for the duration," Tealy had stated, still obviously upset that her mother had no immediate plans to return to Boston. Tealy, nevertheless, had to admit the place felt like a little bit of heaven as she joined both CeCe and Poppy and bared her feet for the sand. She decided even if she was chilly with no socks and shoes, it would still be better than to carry that much sand from the beach, back inside the cottage. Not that it appeared to matter though as Tealy did notice the surprising way her mother lived so freely. She was completely opposite at the townhouse. There would never be a bra on the hardwood floor in the midst of sand granules. How her mother's suitcase had yet to be unpacked was very unlike her as well. She had let so many things *just be* at the cottage. *Little did anyone else know the full extent of her newfound carefree mindset.*

Tealy shoved her hands into the front pocket of her pale pink hoodie as she followed CeCe off of the boardwalk. Poppy trailed behind and put on a pair of sunglasses after she watched her girls do the same. CeCe's pricey Ray-Bans had been perched up on top of her head in her long dark hair since the moment she arrived on island. She even ate breakfast with those sunglasses substituting as a clip to hold back her hair. Tealy, on the contrary, had short hair but full bangs which blew in the wind and nearly covered her shaded eyes. Poppy watched her push the hair back and shift it to one side. *Her girls. So different, and so beautiful in their own unique way.*

Poppy sunk her cherry red toenails in the sand. She noticed CeCe's were a perfectly polished shade of dark blue. And Tealy's were sans polish and all natural once she slipped off her shoes and socks. Having three children had taken an obvious toll on Tealy. She took very little time to pamper herself anymore. Even yoga had taken a backseat, but her cute little curvy figure remained. *The luck of youth*, Poppy thought.

"The sun already feels good out there," CeCe commented as they all three walked, side by side of each other with Poppy sandwiched in the middle.

"It sure does," Poppy agreed, knowing the first dozen steps out there would place them where she wanted to stop walking and talk. After making those strides, Poppy paused for a long while before she spoke. "It was right here. Your grandma took off down the beach to pay our caretaker bill. My grandparents had not stayed with us that summer. They were on a cruise ship the day we packed up to leave for Boston. Bobby and I were sad to leave, but excited to get back home to our friends again. We missed our summers with them, but we knew not going along to the cottage was out of the question — even if our father never joined us." Both CeCe and Tealy were listening raptly. They had heard this story more than once as children, but to actually be standing on the beach, by the ocean where their mother's little brother drowned, was surreal. "There was a cocker spaniel that Bobby had fallen in love with on this beach. It belonged to the family in the cottage two down from ours, right over there," Poppy pointed. "Its fur was a mix of white and caramel brown. It was so tiny, and loveable. Bobby talked about that dog, Timmy nonstop. And when he spotted it getting too close to the water, he froze. He and I both watched the dog abruptly be taken from the shore and enveloped by the tide. It happened in a split second. Bobby ran. I followed him, but not into the water. I stood on the shore where the waves washed up to my knees. At first, I wasn't worried. I could see Bobby. He couldn't see Timmy though, that's why he swam out further. He had his eyes open, searching, and his heart set on saving him.

By that point, I panicked. I started to see the danger in what was happening. I called Bobby back. Over and over, I begged. He was screaming and crying in the water right before he went under." Poppy paused. She lifted her sunglasses off of her face and wiped away the tears that fell as she spoke.

"Mom, you don't have to do this," Tealy interjected. As a child and now an adult, she never could stand to see her mother cry.

"Oh but she does," CeCe corrected her sister. "If this is where you need to retell the story again, we're listening. We are also willing to keep on walking and not force you to relive it. Do what you need to do for you, mom. Not for us. We are big girls."

Poppy smiled. CeCe was straightforward and faced her fears head on. Tealy, Poppy's baby, was more sensitive and guarded with her emotions. She protected her own feelings and most of the time the feelings of others, whereas CeCe looked out for herself. Two girls, raised in the same townhouse on Maple Street in Boston, Massachusetts, could not have been more different. Poppy loved and admired them equally for those unique characteristics.

"I've never again in my life felt so helpless. I remember I froze before I screamed for help. People came, from all directions, including my mother. But there was nothing. The police. The divers. How could they all come up empty-handed? Is the ocean bottomless? We never had his body to say goodbye to." Poppy's daughters had not known this. That fact only added to the horror of the story. "He was wearing a red baseball cap. I've seen that cap every day since, in my mind and sometimes in reality. That cap never surfaced. My brother never survived the depths of that dangerous water. My mother blamed me. I really believed she hated me for not protecting him." Both CeCe and Tealy let their mother speak. They didn't want to know that as a child she had felt to blame, and then unloved years following tragedy. CeCe and Tealy credited Poppy for being a wonderful mother. She could have been quite the opposite, all things considered.

"I can't imagine losing one of my kids," Tealy spoke, batting the tears back from her eyes, and realizing that she missed them and the exhaustingly wonderful days of being a young, busy mother. "I can almost see how grandma gave up."

"Don't make excuses for her," Poppy nearly scolded, but she kept her calm. "I was still alive. I was just a child. And I needed her. I wanted to keep Bobby's memory alive, but she wouldn't allow me to."

"It's not too late, mom," CeCe chimed in. "Start a foundation in his name, donate to animal rescue. I don't see it as you haven't kept his memory alive. He's real to us because you've talked about him so much. The pictures that you still have in frames at home were part of our childhood. To be honest, mom, there were times in my life when I would send up a prayer to heaven and ask Uncle Bobby to have my back. I was probably up to no good in my wild years then, but I wanted to believe he was my guardian angel."

Poppy opened her arms to CeCe. "Thank you," Poppy whispered, as she embraced her eldest daughter, the one she always thought failed at open communication. This was a gift today from her. A much-needed one. Tealy stood there in the sand, and watched the two of them with a pang of jealousy. She was the baby, the daughter who had given her parents their grandchildren first. She gave her son her late uncle's name. She was Poppy's pick. She had always done everything right in her mother's eyes. CeCe was all about spouting empty words — when she eventually made time for her family — and certainly no action. Tealy's children hardly even knew their aunt. She lavished them with expensive birthday and Christmas gifts, but she was never really there and interactive in their lives.

Poppy parted from CeCe and turned to Tealy. Tealy had her arms folded across her chest. Poppy would have recognized that pout paired with a stubborn, defiant stance from miles down the beach. And she knew how to ignore it, too. "Come on, girls. Let's walk."

※ ※ ※

A couple hours after their beach stroll and time spent sitting on the boardwalk in lounge chairs, sipping Bloody Marys (Poppy's idea after she darted off to the kitchen, leaving her girls outside while she prepared their cocktails), they talked of going into town for lunch. They debated between Lookout Tavern, a pub setting with seafood and sushi, or Among the Flowers Café, which served American food and was known for its sweet crepes. CeCe had searched on her cell phone for lunch restaurants on the Vineyard, because Poppy wasn't sure the places she remembered had still existed. Making those small decisions like – *where to go for lunch,* and wasting the day away in the beautiful weather – *with a little vodka in their bloodstream,* were brand new, sweet memories made at the cottage. Poppy already wanted to suggest making the cottage at least an annual place for the three of them to revisit. It was her place now, after all. Poppy imagined taking her grandchildren to the beach for the first time, seeing Tealy and Grant walk hand-in-hand near the water. They were an adorable couple. She even went as far as to visualize CeCe with a special man in her life. One day that would happen, Poppy knew. Her daughter had a lot to offer. She just needed to allow people in, to take the risk. Love was worth it. Even after pain, Poppy still believed that. She saw so much of Reed in CeCe. The need to be loved, the ache for power and prestige. Behind the camera, CeCe felt in control. Poppy understood her more than she realized. And come to find out like her father, Poppy often wondered if CeCe had something to hide. Poppy never pushed her, but she had sensed that there was more to her daughter than she revealed.

CeCe placed her phone on the seat of her lounge chair. "You two decide. My vote is Lookout Tavern. Be right back." When CeCe escaped to empty her bladder, Poppy told Tealy it didn't matter to her where they ate for lunch. "What's your choice?" Poppy asked her.

"Among the Flowers. Let's do crepes for dessert!" It wasn't for the catchy name, the menu, and or even the sweet dessert. The choice in Tealy's mind was simple – she would pick the opposite of her sister, and then make her mother choose sides. *Who's it going to be, mom? CeCe or me?*

"Oh wonderful, now I'm in the middle," Poppy giggled, and didn't appear the least bit rattled. It was only lunch.

"You tell us where we're going," Tealy said, and her mother knew she was being ornery. *That was entirely how Tealy could act when she wanted to get her way.* Tealy stood up from her chair, and stated that she was going inside for her socks and shoes.

Poppy shook her head and smiled from behind her dark sunglasses. When Tealy closed the cottage door, Poppy heard CeCe's cell phone buzz on her empty lounge chair. The screen was face up, and Poppy naturally caught herself glancing at it. There was picture on the screen. It was of a man's legs from the knees down in the sand, with ocean water in the distance. A beach somewhere warm, probably warmer than the fifty-eight degrees Martha's Vineyard was relishing. Poppy didn't intend to pry. She was never good at being nosy or intrusive. Maybe if she had been, she would have caught on to Reed's deception. Without opening the text, which Poppy saw was from Stu Brentwood, she could read, *I wish you were here with me instead.*

Poppy quickly and purposefully dropped the phone back onto the chair. *Stu Brentwood? Jen's brand new husband?* Poppy adored her daughter's lifelong best friend. She had been invited to her wedding just days ago, but had not gone as she was already on island. *Stu wished CeCe was on his honeymoon with him? What in the hell was her daughter doing with her life?*

She thought of Reed. Selfish to the point of being deceptive. *All for sex, or love? How would Poppy stand by and allow her daughter to ruin lives, including her own?*

Still alone on that boardwalk, sitting on her lounge chair beside the two empty ones, Poppy slouched down and looked, through her dark sunglasses, out to the ocean view. She was so troubled by this apparent affair. *CeCe did have a life beyond her career. A lover…who belonged to her best friend. Deception. Betrayal. It couldn't be true.* Poppy felt that familiar sick feeling in the pit of her stomach. *CeCe was her father's daughter.*

Poppy took in a deep breath. She had to pull herself together before her girls returned. She needed to come to a conclusion of how she would handle this news. A text came through that she was not supposed to see, but she had, and there was no way she could do nothing. The fishing dock caught her eye immediately. He was wearing his red cap. She couldn't tell if he had his fishing gear along, or not. He was just sitting there, and this time he was not facing the water. He was facing the cottage, and her. Poppy stared back and did not move. She felt relieved to be somewhat hidden and protected behind her large, dark sunglasses. A strange sensation overtook her body. *Why would she want to feel protected from a man like Dudley?* She was being silly and ridiculous. He was lonely, and probably just watching her and wondering what it would be like when they met up again. *Would the conversation come as easily? Would they succumb to passion, or was that intensity a one-time craze?* Poppy never moved a muscle. She could have nonchalantly lifted her arm in the air and waved her hand. She chose not to. She was certain she already had Dudley's attention. He was, after all, watching *her* out there.

When the cottage door swung open, both of her girls exited. They were ready for lunch, and Poppy was suddenly eager to get out of there with them.

Chapter nine

At Lookout Tavern, the three of them were seated immediately for lunch. They opted not to dine on the waterfront as the air felt cooler than it had earlier. The midday sky was cloudier, and without the warm sun, Tealy made the decision that it was too chilly to eat outside. She was miffed at Poppy for choosing CeCe's restaurant choice over hers, but once she sampled the food on her plate, her mood lightened. *Amazing* was how Tealy described the creamy lobster bisque and sautéed lobster tacos. Poppy chose the New England clam chowder and the fisherman's platter complete with whole belly clams, cold scallops and shrimp. Since her girls arrived on island, Poppy had been eating well. She had an appetite again. She was content to have them with her.

Poppy watched CeCe pick at the cob salad she ordered. The mixed greens were topped with sliced chicken breasts, bacon bits, blue cheese crumbles, sliced egg, tomatoes and avocado. It looked somewhat healthier than what Poppy and Tealy had ordered, and CeCe said it was *delicious*. Even still, Poppy was now looking for signs. *Was she unhappy? Heart-broken? Guilt ridden?* If she and Stu Brentwood were lovers, of course her daughter would be close to distraught right now as he had just married another woman. Not just any woman though. *Mrs. Jen Brentwood was CeCe's best friend for chrissakes.*

The rest of today and all of tomorrow was all of the time Poppy had left with her girls before they would return to Boston. She had to talk to CeCe, and soon.

The high tables and chairs inside the pub were all placed fairly close together. The lunch crowd was loud. Tealy seemed to have relaxed and loosened up with food in her belly. She was smiling now as she told them the story of her second child, Hannah's first day of kindergarten. She had worn a nametag home from school and when Tealy helped her unpeel the white sticker, with HANNAH written in black Sharpie, from the left breast on her chest, Tealy had asked her little girl if she needed to keep the nametag and wear it to school again tomorrow. Hannah had replied, "Oh no, I'm not going back there." Poppy laughed the loudest at that story. Of her three grandchildren, Hannah was the one with the keen sense of humor and big personality. Poppy wore a wide smile on her face at the table with her girls. This trip, her escape to Martha's Vineyard, had taken a happy turn.

Poppy casually glanced toward windows, all along the back wall of the restaurant. It was an inviting view of the waterfront. There were several tables of people dining out there. *It wasn't too chilly for them.* Poppy scanned the view as she had already pushed her plate forward and requested a take-home container for the leftovers. Her daughters were still nibbling on the last of what they wanted to eat from their plates. They were all drinking iced water with lemon since this morning they indulged in more than one Bloody Mary. Poppy picked up her glass just as she spotted him outside, through the window. Water beads were dripping down the exterior of the glass, and it instantly slipped out of her hand, tipped, and spilled over on the table. She up righted it quickly and grabbed her napkin to dab the spill.

"Are you okay, mom?" CeCe asked, offering her napkin to help soak up the water.

"Your face has absolutely no color right now!" Tealy added, trying to keep her voice down so they wouldn't draw more attention to themselves. It had been loud enough in the restaurant for the ruckus to pretty much go unnoticed.

"I'm fine. My fingers just slipped on the outside of my glass — where it's wet," Poppy declared, as she willed herself to regain her composure.

It took a moment for her girls to resume their conversation. CeCe kept sending recurring glances across the table at her mother. *Something was going on with her.* And Tealy was again wrapped up in another story about her children. This one, her seven-year-old oldest daughter, Willow, was the subject. It was blatantly obvious how much Tealy missed her children. Poppy mentally prepared herself to nonchalantly look out of the back window again. She didn't want to make it obvious, if he was still there, that she had seen him. She did, however, need to look again. She was startled the first time. Now, she was ready.

His red cap stood out to her. *Or maybe that was just how Poppy felt about red caps in general?* He was alone at a table for two. He had a plate of food, a longneck bottle of beer. He had been looking away, out toward the water, as Poppy stared. But earlier, Dudley was turned completely around, looking over the back of his chair and into the restaurant — directly at Poppy. This unnerved her more than seeing him stare at her on the boardwalk. She knew he followed her and the girls to lunch. Poppy attempted to chalk this up to loneliness, and it justly could very well be. He was keeping his distance from her at the cottage while her girls were on island, but he kept showing up. Nearby. *Did he want her to know he was there? Was this some kind of possessive, obsessive behavior?* Poppy concluded that she needed to relax. She suggested they stop by the market on their way back to the cottage — for some dinner ingredients and more wine.

✄ ✄ ✄

It was unexpected and alarming. And not to mention disappointing. They had just returned to the cottage and the three of them were in the kitchen unpacking their groceries bags from the market. Poppy teased them about having just stocked her cabinets and refrigerator one day earlier. Tealy told her they didn't eat the same things as she did, and CeCe called their mother out on just needing to pick up more wine. They were giggling when Tealy's cell phone rang in the front pocket of her pale pink hoodie. She stated that it was her husband, Grant before she answered.

Poppy and CeCe stopped putting the groceries away and stood listening to their end of Tealy's phone conversation.

Okay, well how high is the fever?

Did you call the pediatrician?

How long ago did you give him Motrin?

Yes, I can hear him crying.

Grant, I just got here today. I'll be home tomorrow night.

You're making me feel awful.

I know he wants his mommy. I want to hold him, too.

CeCe finally interjected. She had driven them from Boston, to the ferry, and then onto to Martha's Vineyard. Sisters or not, CeCe realized that Tealy felt stuck without a vehicle there on the island. CeCe was actually waiting for her little sister to demand that they leave now. *Give me a ride back home!* But, she hadn't yet. Tealy appeared to not want to leave. Maybe as a seasoned mother she had not seen any urgency to her baby having a fever. CeCe was trying to read her emotions while she spoke on the phone to her husband. Finally, CeCe just said, "You can take my car. I'll have mom bring me to the ferry tomorrow night, and after it docks in Boston, I'll take a cab to your house."

"You would do that for me?" Tealy asked, feeling loved, but also irked at the thought of CeCe getting to enjoy another twenty-four hours of what was supposed to be *their* trip. She was jealous of the time CeCe would now have alone at the cottage, with their mother. Tealy forced herself to concentrate on her baby. *Think of your son!*

"Of course. Grab your bag!" CeCe barked at her. "Mom, can you follow us?" CeCe was planning ahead for a ride back to the cottage after they saw Tealy off. Poppy nodded. She could have cried. She didn't want their two days together to end so abruptly. Nonetheless, she was proud of her children. Tealy was a wonderful mother. And CeCe really could be a supportive sister when she wanted to.

Chapter ten

Poppy drove alone, following close behind her girls. CeCe drove like a bat out of hell, which forced Poppy to sit up a little taller, grip the steering wheel tighter, and give the gas pedal on her sliver sedan some serious acceleration.

When they reached the ferry dock, Poppy parked her car in the lot as CeCe and Tealy were in the long line to get Tealy a spot on the next ferry. It was last-minute, so they were in the midst of a bumper to bumper crowd of vehicles.

A ticket was purchased, and CeCe and Tealy had just gotten out of CeCe's vehicle. Tealy was going to take the driver's seat, immediately after they said goodbye. Poppy was standing near them now.

She watched her girls share a quick embrace, and heard Tealy say *thank you, again.* And then Poppy stepped up to her youngest daughter. She opened her arms to Tealy. She enveloped her into the arms that loved her, and worried about her — even as a grown woman.

"Those babies of yours are incredibly lucky to have you," Poppy told Tealy as she noticed the tears welling up in her eyes. "Go take care of them. I'll be fine." Poppy knew that Tealy's concern for her was real as she had been alone on the island and back at the cottage which held a tragic childhood memory for her. Poppy hoped after spending a little there with her, Tealy would be confident in Poppy's ability to handle this. Poppy's wish was for her daughters to see her as a strong woman, and believe that they also shared the same trait.

"I want to come back," Tealy sniffed as she spoke, and for a moment she was a little girl again in Poppy's embrace.

"You can. This will be the first of many visits. Next time, bring Grant and my grandbabies." Poppy smiled, and this time she was the one crying. The idea of her daughter wanting to be on island, as she personally had so many times as a child, absolutely made Poppy's return there feel like the right thing.

✝ ✝ ✝

Poppy drove back to the cottage with CeCe in her passenger seat this time.

"I feel sorry for Tealy," CeCe stated, and Poppy took her eyes off of the road to look at her. "Kids, babies…you just have no life once they are in your life. I mean, Jesus, she couldn't even enjoy one night, two days max, away from them."

"It's a sacrifice a woman makes when she becomes a mother. You ought to consider it sometime," Poppy told her thirty-one-year-old child. She never implied that CeCe wasn't getting any younger, but she thought it. Her biological clock was ticking. And she wanted to tell her to live her life with no regrets. *Don't miss your chance to have a baby.* And while her thoughts unraveled, she also wanted to say, *Don't claim someone else's man.* She and CeCe were sure to have that conversation now that they were going to be alone at the cottage. It was inevitable. It needed to be put out there, discussed, and dealt with. Poppy took it as a sign that Tealy was called away. Tealy's interference with that secret would not have been a positive thing. Poppy knew that Tealy would have accused her sister of being just like their father. While Poppy had thought it, she would not say it. She promised herself that already.

"I'm not cut out to love anyone else more than myself," CeCe spoke. At first, Poppy let out a slight giggle. And then she realized CeCe was being completely serious. "My job is like my baby. I've grown along with it, I've nurtured it. I adore it. I cannot imagine my life not doing what I do."

Poppy nodded her head. Although she was never a career woman, she somewhat understood. She had lived with Reed for twenty-eight years, and had heard so much of the same from him. His career as an oral surgeon often times had given Poppy the feeling that she and her girls were second best to his precious dentistry world. Turns out, they were second best to his other family as well.

"What about love? A lover? Your video camera and editing equipment cannot bring you that kind of fulfillment, can it?" Luckily, they were just minutes from arriving at the cottage, because this conversation had already turned entirely too serious to have in a moving vehicle.

CeCe chuckled. "Seriously mom? Are we having the talk now? Fifteen years too late?" Poppy did her best to teach her girls good values about sex when they were teenagers. Their conversations had always been awkward though. Poppy didn't seem embarrassed now, and that actually made CeCe feel like hiding underneath the front seat of the car.

"I've never been comfortable talking about sex," *and doing it,* Poppy thought. Until Dudley just one night ago. Poppy was fifty-three years old and never before had she felt so in tune with her own body. It was strange, but that one intimate experience had given her the courage to have this conversation with her daughter. And to confront her about the text she accidently intercepted.

"I'm a grown woman, mother," CeCe stated as they parked in the lot near the cottage. Now that they were back, CeCe wanted to get out of the car and escape this topic. "I assure you, I have sex, I enjoy it. I just don't need a husband and babies — like my sister. We have always been different, and we are opposites in that regard too."

Poppy followed CeCe up to the cottage in silence. They kicked off their sand-covered flip flops when they walked over the threshold. When Poppy closed the door, she spoke again. "Who are you having sex with?" At first, Poppy thought, *what kind of question was that?* She really had no right to ask that of

86

her daughter. And that's exactly how she would have felt if CeCe had turned the question around on her. What she and Dudley did was private.

CeCe laughed out loud. "I can't believe my ears. Do you want me to make a list? Do you want to hear about the time when we were on location for a shoot and I gave the camera man on my team a blowjob, and he in turn gave me—"

"Stop right there," Poppy held up her hand in front of her daughter. "There is no need for you to react this way. I've never pried, I've never asked you about your sex life, or lack of. I had just hoped you weren't lonely and you were feeling loved the way a woman should."

"The way dad loved you?" CeCe snapped. She never should have said that, but she felt uncomfortable and angry with her mother right now, and this was her way of lashing out.

"That's not fair," Poppy replied. "He did love me. He just did not honor me."

"I'm sorry. I shouldn't have—" CeCe tried to apologize.

"It's fine," Poppy stopped her. "I'm just going to ask you something, straight out," Poppy said, as she paced behind the white suede sofa while CeCe remained standing at one end of it. "Your phone was on the lounge chair outside earlier. A text came through and I didn't mean to, but I saw it. I read it."

CeCe's eyes widened, and then Poppy watched her compose herself. She knew which text her mother was referring to. Stu had told her he was only going to be able to get away from work for a few days, at most, but he had planned to take his wife some place warm for a brief honeymoon. "I could talk my way out of this one, mother. I could say that Stu Brentwood and I go way back as friends. We're more than that though. We were together long before Jen ever met and fell head over heels for the man in my bed."

Oh my God. So it was true. Poppy stayed silent. She searched her mind, and her heart, for the exact words to say. She wanted to say the right thing. She needed to. Her daughter's life was spiraling out of control — and given Poppy's experience with cheaters, she truly wanted no part of offering sound advice. She was appalled by cheaters. She ran from that kind of dishonesty and deception, and never looked back. She loathed what it had done to her life. But she would not disown or judge her daughter. She only wanted to kick her ass, and hopefully some sense into her in the process. What CeCe was doing was mindless and heartless.

"For how long?" Poppy asked her daughter.

"What does it matter, mom?" CeCe was going to shut down. But Poppy refused to allow it.

"Oh it matters!" Poppy immediately responded. "I'm sure it will matter to Jen. She will find out. You know that, right? Unless you've ended it, and plan to go to your grave with a secret that deep. Oh wait, look what happened to your father's mistress and mother of his son…she took it to her grave alright!" CeCe deserved that. She stood there and took it like a grown woman. It was Poppy who stopped. She felt overwhelmed, startled. Poppy had done what she promised herself she would not do. CeCe and Reed's actions and reckless choices had made them one in the same. *Was it really necessary to rub that into her daughter's face at the moment?*

"It's not over. No one ended anything," CeCe revealed. "Their marriage doesn't change a damn thing between us."

Poppy did all she could not to let her jaw drop to the floor at her sand-covered feet. "Then why did he choose her? Why did he marry your best friend, instead of you?" That was the real question here.

"Because I said no. I turned down his marriage proposal, long before he offered to share his life with my best friend," CeCe sighed.

"Why? Why would you do that? Why would he do that?" None of this story made sense to Poppy. It was like a badly written novel. It was a story full of nonsense just to fill the pages.

"He wants to run for mayor. His people have been on him to give the public eye a fairytale image with a wife — and babies. That's not me. I do not want to be someone's wife, nor do I need to bore babies. He loves me, but he loves his career more." CeCe didn't flinch as she explained something so outrageous that Poppy believed any moment she would wake up on the sofa in front of her to find it had all been just a dream. Her daughters hadn't shown up at the cottage and she'd still be in the clothes, sans a bra, that Dudley had taken off of her before he took her body and passionately joined it with his.

"So you gave him your blessing? Your approval for him to be with your best friend?" Poppy asked. CeCe nodded. "Explain that to me. Clarify, with details, how someone can betray another person that they claim to love?" This was getting too personal for Poppy. CeCe knew the facts. This issue lied on the most unsteady, shaky ground. *Was this really about CeCe, or were these unspoken emotions that Poppy had refused to ever truly face head on?*

"It's never about the person you love, the person you're hurting," CeCe began to explain. "It's about yourself. It's about me. It's about how I feel when I'm with a man who gives me what I need. Before Jen was in the picture, and while she's been in his life, I have felt the very same. I want only what I have, moment to moment, with Stu. Nothing more. Jen wants all of him, and she can have him and the entirety of marriage and babies. I just need my part of him."

"Do you hear yourself?" Poppy scolded her with an accusatory question. "That is not normal. You deserve more. You cannot believe that a man, coming around occasionally for sex, is how you will be content living for the rest of your life! And can you imagine your life without your best friend, poor and innocent Jen? Because, my dear child, that will happen. It may have taken too blasted decades, but your father's secret was discovered. And, if you ask me, it ruined him. Look at him sometime. Take a good, long look at your father. Maybe it's the fact that he was found out? Or maybe it's the cold hard truth that he's now facing life alone." Once again, Poppy felt remorse for making this about Reed.

"I don't want to be alone either," CeCe admitted. "And I'm not. You may think I'm the biggest, cold-hearted bitch on this earth, but I don't have to care. That's your opinion. What I share with Stu is a deep-rooted connection. It's about more than physical attraction. I need him. And I will not give him up. Not for anyone."

Poppy was silent for a long time. It was just her and her oldest daughter in the living room of that cottage. A cottage that withstood several decades of time and had literally weathered storms. Poppy had no doubt they were surrounded and protected by internally battered walls which had heard entirely too much through the years. No family was perfect. No one person was left unscathed of pain and heartache. This wasn't about her daughter just having an affair. This was something more. *But what? Had Poppy somehow failed as a parent? Was CeCe lacking love and affection and appreciation? Had she not respected herself enough to feel worthy of love and marriage and children? Or was this not about Poppy at all?* This could be the blood in CeCe Brennan's veins. The makeup of her DNA. Reed, too, was not a terrible person because of a traumatic childhood or some underlying cause buried deep in his past. But he was a man who had made an unforgivable mistake. Poppy had already thought long and hard about it, about him. She could not change Reed or what he had done to her, nor did she want to after all the pain. But, for her daughter, Poppy would die trying to save her from herself.

Chapter eleven

"Make a promise to me," CeCe requested of her mother as they walked the beach that evening. The air was cooler and both were wearing jackets, zipped entirely up to their necks. "Let me make my own mistakes, just like when I was growing up. My friends were envious because you didn't try to control me. You were there to steer me this way or that way, but ultimately I chose what I wanted to do or what I believed was right for me."

Poppy nodded. *Was she truly in agreement with this?* "You always did have such a way with words," she began. "You're just like your father."

"Are you judging me again?" CeCe asked her mother. Poppy had every right to condemn her husband. But it wasn't justifiable for her to be critical of CeCe for being exactly like her father.

"No, honey. No. And I never meant to before," she said, regretfully. "Reed hurt me so terribly. But the fact is, I love him and probably always will. He, despite everything, has some wonderful qualities. And that's what I meant about you." Poppy took her daughter's hand in hers. "Listen...I've been very good about not beating down the privacy walls you've put up through the years." CeCe was her self-sufficient, independent daughter. "Knowing what I know does explain so much now. You're hiding, you're ashamed. You may not want to admit it, but in your heart you know it's wrong."

"But it is my life," CeCe stated as she took her hand from her mother's and moved closer to her. They locked arms as they walked. CeCe was considerably taller than Poppy, even when both were barefoot. "Haven't you ever done something in your life on impulse and once you're in it, you realize nothing matters but how you feel?" Poppy's mind flashed to Dudley. She wasn't so sure that she could have related to CeCe's question if she hadn't just done something so completely out of character.

"Yes, I have," Poppy all but whispered.

"You're not going to share it with me, are you?" CeCe asked, with a smirk.

She couldn't. It was still so new and fresh. And confusing. "No," was all she said in response.

Saying goodbye to CeCe proved to be much harder than Poppy realized. Maybe it was the fact that she would be alone again. *But wasn't that partly the reason for her retreat to the cottage?*

Poppy drove her to the ferry dock and held onto to her a little tighter and a few seconds longer before they parted ways.

"I want more phone calls, texts, videos, whatever it is that you do best," Poppy smiled up at her oldest daughter with tears threatening to spill over from her eyes.

"And I want you to be okay here alone. I personally could handle this place solo for awhile, but I know it holds pain for you. Just don't sit around being sad. Okay?" CeCe squeezed her mother's shoulders one more time.

"I'll be happy if you'll be happy," Poppy bargained.

"Deal."

When Poppy slipped behind the steering wheel of her car, she sat there and watched her daughter walk onto the ferry dock. One day Poppy hoped CeCe wouldn't be walking alone. Or hiding an awful secret. Poppy wondered if there were people in her own life through the years who knew about Reed's secret and purposely kept it from her. If there were, Poppy was now no better than them.

Poppy returned to the cottage with a heavy heart. Her girls were adults with their own lives now. They were making choices, pertinent decisions, without even consulting her. She wasn't needed by them in the same manner she used to be. It's not that Poppy first realized this now. She just suddenly had the haunting issue of being aware that CeCe's actions were going to ruin her life. *Could she really leave this alone? And what then? Would she just stand idle while her firstborn child's life played out to a disaster?*

Going back to Boston didn't seem like the answer right now. Poppy still had her mind set on spending infinite time on island, alone. She smirked at her initial plan to be *alone*. First, there was Dudley. Then, her girls. She marveled about Dudley. She almost wished they could meet again as strangers, in an effort to bypass the awkwardness. *Assuming that it would be uncomfortable to look at each other again and speak after sex between two people who were basically strangers.* And then there was the fact that Poppy had caught him watching her—twice. She accused herself of being ridiculous. It's a small island. *Was ninety-six miles of island considered small?* People shared the same space, like the beach. And they also bumped into each other all the time, like at restaurants and at the market. It's called coincidence. *Get a grip, Poppy. Find something to do. You're over thinking.*

She searched the cottage as if she was suddenly on a mission. She opened closets and drawers. Some of the drawers were empty, and smelled of moth balls or a disinfectant. Poppy had yet to put her clothing and belongings in the dressers or closets. She was living out of her suitcase still, as if she was in a hotel. She never did use the drawer space in hotels or condos either over the years with Reed and their girls. Reed used to laugh at her, living out of her suitcase, when he would always unpack and make himself at home. Maybe that was her problem at the cottage, too. She had yet to truly feel at home. She was getting there though. She could feel the pull. There was history, her family's history, in that cottage on the beachfront.

She walked to the hall closet, past the two bedrooms, and the bathroom at the very end of the hallway. Other than towels and bed linens, there really wasn't anything out of the ordinary stored there. Poppy again wondered who had been there over the years to do the upkeep, the minor remodels, and change of décor and furniture. As she had found out in her mother's will, her parents owned the cottage after the death of her grand-parents. That felt strange, especially knowing her mother had never told her. What a ridiculous way to find out — at the reading of her mother's will. And now Poppy owned this piece of family history.

As she had expected, at first glance, there were basic closet things stored in there. And then she looked a little closer. A sweater jacket hanging on the short rod that spanned wall to wall in that dark closet. The color was winter white, but it had yellowed with time. Like the way father time showed up with wrinkles and aching bones. Time affected absolutely everything in its path. *A sweater jacket.* A front-opened cardigan, made of thick cotton. It was long, meant to fit well past any waistline. Poppy could still see her mother wearing one. *Was this the same one? Was this hers?* If it had been the very same sweater jacket that belonged to her mother, Poppy wondered how on earth it had gotten there. They only visited the cottage in the summer-time. And they had not been back since the summer she was twelve years old. Had her mother owned more than one of those? Was it her grandmother's? *Jesus, that garment was ancient, if so.* Poppy took it off of the hanger and brought it to her nose. It smelled musty. She was certain that her mother had worn it, or one exactly like it. She hadn't forgotten the thick, itchy feel of it, when she was close by her mother. There was just no way her mother had returned to the cottage, during off season or anytime, after her Bobby died. *Was there?*

Poppy attempted to hang up the sweater jacket again, but she lost hold of it and dropped it on the floor at her feet. As she bent down to retrieve it, she saw a clear storage container with a blue lid on the floor of the closet. She could clearly see through side of the bin and noticed pictures in there. Poppy sat down on the floor with the rumpled sweater jacket next to her. She dragged the bin on the floor toward her, and lifted the lid.

Snapshots, some as old as Polaroid's were stacked in there. With technology now, Poppy missed what it truly meant to hold a photograph in her hands. She didn't have prints made often enough from the photos stored in her cell phone gallery. Most of those gallery photos were of her three grandchildren. It's what people did to keep photos with them all of the time, and they were convenient to share that way. Some of the photographs in that bin on the floor in front of her were of people she had no idea who they were, or where most of the moments were captured. Even names handwritten on the back had not been familiar to her. She rooted deeper, and then she saw a photo of her parents when they were young and in love. They looked happy. Probably because those were the carefree days before her father became a judge, and allowed that career to consume him. They also had no children yet. They were just babies themselves. Poppy turned the picture over to see if anything had been written on the backside. *The love of my life. Jon and Julie. 1959.*

Jon and Julie Blare. It's been a long time since Poppy thought of herself as a Blare. For nearly thirty years, she had been a Brennan. She was proud to take Reed's name. Even that felt tarnished now. *How could he have loved another woman and conceived a child with her? And then he had raised a son with her, in secret for all those years.* Poppy forced herself out of those thoughts. Dwelling wouldn't change a thing. She did wonder though if she should have demanded more answers from Reed. After she exposed his secret that godawful day at the funeral home, Poppy had just wanted out. *Shut up and divorce me.*

There were more pictures of her parents together. Many of her grandparents too. They had been gone so long that Poppy almost forgot what they looked like. There was one photograph of them on the front porch of the cottage. Poppy wanted to keep that one, and maybe take it home to her townhouse in Boston. She chose to keep two photographs of her parents, as well. There were faces of people she did not recognize. *More family, or friends,* she assumed. One photograph caught Poppy's eye. It was of her and Bobby. They had to be five and six years old. Nothing was written on the back of the photo. They were on island, on the beach, in front of the cottage. Bobby was standing in the sand with a blue plastic shovel in hand and two pales at his feet, one red and one yellow. Poppy was almost entirely buried in the sand. She smiled, and laughed out loud. She hadn't remembered that day. Bobby's smile, however, which was still vibrant in that old photograph, was something she had never forgotten. *This photo was a keeper, too.*

Poppy found a photo upside down. The handwriting on the back was scribbled, but she could read. *Van Blare. 2010.* That was only seven years ago. Underneath his name and date, he had written, *Thank you, Aunt Julie! Love you the most!* She turned the photograph around and there he was. Van the man, as he liked to call himself. He was six and a half years older than Poppy. In that photo, he had to have been a few years over fifty, as Poppy was now. He looked model perfect in nothing but a pair of swim trunks. His chest was hairless and tight. His abs looked drawn on. His face showed the after effects of loving the sun all of his life. He had crow's feet and laugh lines, but his smile was so wide, teeth incredibly white, and his hair was probably too long for his age, but it looked as golden as Poppy remembered from her youth. A woman had taken the photo of him, Poppy could tell, because she had gotten her finger in the way. There was a long pale pink polished nail, a pinky bent at the knuckle, on the top left corner of the photo. She was probably a fling for him, Poppy thought, or maybe his third wife — since the photo that was taken was fairly recent. *Had this photo ever reached her mother?* It was obviously for her, but since it was in a bin with other photographs at the cottage that her mother never returned to, Poppy believed not. She flipped the photograph over again. At the bottom, she now first noticed, that Van —or someone— had written what looked like a phone number. Poppy put that photograph aside, also on the keep pile.

⚡⚡⚡

Poppy attempted to search through more of the photographs as she sat on the floor at the end of the hallway, in front of the open closet door. Her mind kept going back to the small pile of visual memories in front of her. Her grandparents were long gone from this earth, and now her parents were both gone forever too. Poppy had her daughters and her grandchildren in her life now. She had kept in very little contact with her family. She just saw a few of them who came to her mother's funeral a half a year ago already. Van had been one of them. She tried to recall their conversations. He had arrived in Boston alone, not that Poppy would have cared if he had a woman on his arm. His father, Cruz Blare, who was Poppy's uncle and her mother's younger brother, was in ill health, and Van had gotten him out of the nursing home to attend the funeral. She remembered now that Van had told her if she ever needed anything, to call him. Poppy started to get up off of the floor. Her knees felt knobby on the hardwood floor and *her lower back had stiffened up a bit sitting for too long.* "Sucks to get old," she spoke aloud, and giggled —because she was hardly old.

She found her cell phone resting on the back of the white suede sofa. She hadn't heard it sound off, but there was a message from CeCe, letting her know she arrived at Tealy's house by cab to get her car. There was a selfie attached of both of her girls, along with her three grandbabies. CeCe was holding Baby Keegan. Poppy smiled. *One day, my big girl will have one of those of her own. I'm sure of it. You're going to get your life on track. You have to. You only get one. Don't screw it up.* Poppy saved that picture to the gallery on her cell phone.

She sent CeCe a reply. *Thank you for letting me know you made it safely. Kiss those precious babies for me. Tealy too. Call me soon. xoxo*

With her phone still in hand, Poppy searched her contacts on the list all the way down to the Vs. She also had the photograph from the closet of her cousin Van in her hand. Those two phone numbers were a match. She would call him.

Poppy wasn't sure why exactly, but she felt compelled to. Maybe he could answer a few questions for her. Like, for starters, *has anyone other than him been staying at the cottage over the years?* And, maybe, *did one of his lady friends leave behind a sweater jacket?* That made Poppy laugh. She doubted a woman, Van's type, with Botox and fake boobs, would be caught wearing anything remotely old lady-ish.

Chapter twelve

Poppy thought about just sending a text. It was simpler. If she were interrupting him, he could choose to ignore her and get back with her when it was convenient. A phone call would demand his attention now. *Maybe that's what she preferred? Maybe it was now or never, time to ask some questions she should have asked awhile ago.* Poppy dialed Van's number.

Two rings later, a male voice answered. "This is Van."

"Hello Van, it's Poppy. Your cousin."

"Of course there's only one Poppy Seed! How in the world are you, beautiful girl?" Poppy smiled. The charmer. The thrice married playboy who she called her cousin, but didn't really know at all.

"I'm doing well. I'm on island, actually, and I thought of you," Poppy admitted.

"No? Wait. You, seriously, are at the cottage?" Van voice seemed to humanize from big and bad to just a man, concerned about a family member. It could have been Poppy's imagination, but she thought not.

"I am. First time back in over forty years."

"Holy shit. You okay there?" Van paused. "Look, I heard about your husband. Um, I don't know what to say. That's partly why I never called you. I'm an ass. I like my women too, so I'm not sure you would have believed I was being sincere if I called to say I was sorry to hear…"

"It's fine. You're fine," Poppy cut him off mid-explanation. "I am okay here. It wasn't easy, but I like it here. The cottage just feels like home to me."

"Ah, yeah, I get that. Aunt Julie was such a gem to let me stay whenever I asked," Van stated.

"About that," Poppy began. "So were you the only person in our family, or otherwise, to stay here for reoccurring trips?"

"I think so, other than Aunt Julie. I mean, I never stayed at the same time she was on island." Poppy was instantly confused by Van's words.

"What? I don't understand," Poppy spoke into the phone, as she walked around to the front of the sofa, and sat down. She never leaned back. She kept both of her feet firmly planted on the floor in front of her as she sat on the edge of the white suede sofa. She was beginning to like that sofa so much. The softness was a comfort of home. She didn't have suede furniture at the townhouse, nor did she ever think she would like it. It may have not even been the sofa's texture or anything close, Poppy realized, it was most likely just being there. She had missed so much about that part of her life.

"Aunt Julie visited the cottage, it was hers after our grandparents died," Van started to explain.

"I actually just found out that she owned it for years and, well, now I do. It was bequeathed to me in my mother's will. She never told me. We didn't speak of the cottage after Bobby died."

There was silence on the opposite end of the phone for a moment. "Well I guess I should be pissed that she never left it to me, considering I was the only one who cared about visiting it as much as her," Van chuckled. "My second wife actually redecorated the place. Julie paid for it, she insisted." That was one question answered. *There weren't drastic changes in the décor, but it had been modernized nonetheless.*

Poppy wanted to tell him that the *cottage looks great,* and maybe thank him or one of his ex wives, but first she had to address what he said about her mother. It was almost as if Poppy had already known. *The sweater jacket hanging in the hall closet.*

"My mother returned to the cottage after my brother died?" It was a simple question, with an answer that was going to complicate Poppy's understanding of everything.

"Hell yes," Van spoke with certainty. "She needed that place. She always came alone though. She was very clear with me about no one else knowing. Not your father. And not you."

"Why?" Poppy asked, with adamancy in her voice. She needed to know. *She had a right to know!* But her poor cousin Van most likely didn't have all the answers she sought.

"Healing, she used to say," Van offered. "Look, I'm sorry Poppy Seed. I loved my aunt, but she could be a cold battle ax when she wanted to be. I didn't want to cross her."

Poppy sighed, "I'll say. It's not your worry, Van. Thank you for telling me. I mean, as far as I know, no one in my house knew that my mother ever came back here." Poppy really had no clue whether her father had known or not. She also recalled her mother going out of town *to visit family* as a common reoccurrence. Those must have been the times she was on island, at the cottage Poppy missed beyond words. *Why hadn't her mother taken her along?* Instead, and alone, it had taken Poppy more that forty years to build up the courage to return.

"If you're alone and you need someone to hold you up, I can come and be there for you, Poppy Seed." It was a kind thought and a sweet offer, but the last thing Poppy needed was to convert the cottage into a frat house. Van wouldn't last long without a woman. She thought of Dudley and herself doing the deed on the floor behind the sofa. *Maybe she already had a jump-start on the party.*

"Van, you're the sweetest, but no. I need to do this by myself. Being here is therapeutic for me. I'm sure of it." Poppy held her breath. She really didn't need anyone else showing up, uninvited or unannounced.

"You're just like your mother," Van spoke.

"Really, Van? Do you want me to come through this phone and kick your ass!" Poppy heard him roar with laughter. She pulled her phone away from her ear for a moment. And she giggled.

"Right!" he laughed again. "I gotcha. Who the Sam hell wants to be compared to anyone in *our* family?"

"Exactly," Poppy agreed. "Listen Van, you were a great help. I just needed to know if she was here, ever, and now I know more than I expected to. Thank you."

"Anytime, Poppy Seed."

✗ ✗ ✗

So she was now aware that her mother had spent decades returning to the cottage, probably right after Bobby was gone, and then repeatedly for years long after. It angered her. Poppy would have given anything to come back to this place. And to not have to do it alone, four decades later, when her own life had been ripped apart at the seams. *Damn you, Julie Blare. You weren't my mother after Bobby died.*

Poppy stood up abruptly from the sofa. She caught herself pacing in circles. She wanted to search for something more in that cottage. In every nook and cranny. *Was there more to find? More to tell?* Poppy felt as if she was on a scavenger hunt from hell. It was torture for her to know her mother secretly returned to the cottage. It was selfish of her. *Wasn't it?* Poppy had no other explanation for it.

She was enthralled in her thoughts. She wanted a glass of wine or a walk on the beach to calm her nerves. Through the window blinds, she could see the sun was beginning to set. Maybe she would walk in the dark, or wait until the morning. That glass of wine seemed more appealing by the second. Her back was to the front door as she walked toward the kitchen. Two knocks stopped her.

And from the other side of the door, she heard, "Poppy... It's Dudley."

Chapter thirteen

Poppy froze. Naturally, she stopped everything. He could not have been farther from her thoughts right now. She was caught up in her past, her present, and not at all concerned about her future. *Was Dudley her future?* That was the very last thing she wanted to think about. She felt miffed as she stepped toward the door. She wanted to be left alone. Those what ifs and nervous vibes also started to push to the surface. *Who was this man, really?*

She caught herself opening the door slowly. On the other side of it, Dudley stood there. Black baseball cap. Baggy faded jeans. Gray jacket, zipped all the way up. Flip flops. And he wore a wide smile. "Is the coast clear?" he asked her, but it was as if he already knew both of her daughters had left the island.

Poppy smiled, but she realized it didn't feel genuine. "All alone am I," she responded, as she remained standing in the doorway. *Did he want her to invite him inside?*

"I just wanted to say I'm sorry if I overstepped with the flowers," he stated, referring to the half dozen long-stemmed yellow roses that were still the centerpiece on her kitchen table. She hadn't been very good about remembering to water them. CeCe took care of that for the two days she was there.

"No need to apologize, and you covered our tracks well in front of my girls." *Our? Was there an our? An us?*

"Good," Dudley said, smiling again. Poppy thought of him as eighteen again, standing there thinking about what they had done, and possibly feeling horny and hoping to come back for more. *Oh my.* This wasn't fair. Poppy had wanted what happened between them to happen —then and there— just as much as Dudley had. She believed they were both caught off guard by their out of control emotions.

The wind picked up, and Poppy immediately noticed the air temperature was cooling off as nightfall approached. Dudley winced and reached for his jacket pockets with both of his hands.

"It's getting cold," she noted. "Do you—"

"Want to come inside?" he interrupted her. "That's not why I stopped by. I don't want to overwhelm you, or take up your time. I guess I just hoped we could start over."

"Start over?" Poppy asked him. *Had he had the very same thought she did? The one about wishing they could meet again, before they had sex, and take everything slower. Whatever this thing was.*

Dudley nodded. Poppy stepped back. And then she heard herself say, "Come inside."

He stepped in and closed the door behind him. They both already felt better being on the other side of the weather. The close of one door had brought them some form of comfort. The at-ease feeling between them, however, was still out there somewhere.

They stood in the living room, uncomfortably close to where they both consented to lose control for a little while.

"There's still so much we really do not know about each other," Poppy began, as Dudley took his hands out of his jacket pockets. He knew the shocking reason why she was divorced. He wasn't aware that her happy childhood had ended once her brother died. And now she had just discovered that her mother had lied to her. The woman, who Poppy believed couldn't face her grief, had been back to the cottage. Poppy was so angry with her she could have screamed until she cried. *Did she really want to involve a man with her life as it was — in shambles?*

"We probably should have had more conversations before we..." Dudley stopped speaking any further. Even in their fifties, sex was still awkward to talk about at times.

110

"I liked being with you, Dudley," Poppy tried to lift and lead this conversation to exactly where it needed to go. "I believe that neither one of us is to blame, more than the other, for initiating what happened. It just happened. You are in the throes of brand new grief. I am a mess of emotions right now, for reasons you are not even aware of. It just felt right to be in that moment."

Dudley nodded his head. "I agree, I completely agree with all you've said. I walked away feeling guilty as I thought of my wife. I don't treat a woman that way. I court her first, or at least that's what I did with my wife." His wife was still so much on his mind. Poppy felt sorry for him as she spoke of her, but hearing the words *my wife* repeatedly had suddenly made her feel like an intrusive whore. Dudley's wife was gone. Poppy slept with a man who was a widower. She did absolutely nothing wrong. "I would like to see you again. We can make a pact…to keep our clothes on."

He looked nervous to Poppy. As nervous as she felt right now. "I'm sure we will be seeing a lot of each other on this island," she started to say.

"Have dinner with me tonight. I know it's getting late. Have you eaten yet?" Dudley suddenly appeared assertive to her.

"I really didn't plan for anything," she told him. She just wanted that drink. She wanted to escape this moment and go into the kitchen to grab a bottle of wine by its neck, and maybe take the time to pour a glass. Or maybe she would swig it straight from the bottle.

"So it that a yes…or no?" Dudley asked outright. Again, his assertiveness annoyed her. He seemed impatient with her, and Poppy didn't like feeling pushed.

"No. I'm just not up for conversation tonight." Poppy watched him, as she all but held her breath.

"I understand," he said the words, but not in a way that made Poppy believe him. "I'll check on you tomorrow. Maybe you'll be interested in dinner, or conversation, then?" Dudley looked hopeful. Poppy smiled, but again it didn't feel the least bit genuine.

He backed toward the door. She walked forward to see him out of that door. He stopped. She didn't move anymore either. She was too close right now and needed to take a step back. The last thing she wanted was for this to be déjà vu. Dudley reached up his hand and touched her cheek. He came at her with his mouth on hers. His lips, this time, felt like lips. That's it. There was no passion. Just a man's lips pressed on hers, with his tongue forcing entry. Poppy didn't respond. She didn't like how this felt, or how he tasted. Not at all. It was as if she had been someone else with him when she enjoyed and wanted this before. Her lips were pursed. Her mouth was completely closed. She took both of her hands, placed them on his chest, actually higher as she felt his collar bone underneath her fingers. She didn't hesitate to push him off of her.

"I'm sorry, I shouldn't have. It's just you. You're beautiful. Irresistible, Poppy." Dudley stared. Poppy insides sunk. She was sickened by this. By him.

"You should go," she told him firmly.

"Right," he said. "See you around. Soon, okay?"

Poppy closed the door tight when he stepped outside, onto the front porch. And for the first time since she arrived, and ever at that cottage, she turned the deadbolt to lock the door. She stood by it, realizing in a slight state of panic that Dudley was the caretaker. He had a key to the cottage. He could insert it into the keyhole on that door now and reverse the deadbolt right in front of her eyes.

Like hell was she going to allow him to scare her, or control her.

He was gone now. Poppy retrieved her cell phone, resting on the back of the sofa again, and she did an immediate search for locksmiths on Martha's Vineyard. It was time to change the bolt on the cottage door. The windows would need robust locks as well. And if he came back and tried to force his way in, she would call the police.

Chapter fourteen

After CeCe promised to bring surprises (in the form of toys) the next time she visited, Tealy sent Grant upstairs with all three of their children. He was going to give the baby a bath and then read bedtime stories. He was doing more to help Tealy the past few days. When she returned from a trip to the cottage that was brought to an unexpected halt, Tealy had broken down and admitted to her husband that she was sinking. *She didn't like who she was anymore. Not with him. And not with their family.* It scared him to death, because his best friend's wife had just left him, Grant knew, for the very same reason. A woman could become overwhelmed to the point of wanting out. Grant wouldn't allow that to happen to his wife, and his family. What Tealy needed, he would provide.

"What's with Grant?" CeCe asked Tealy as they stood near the island in the kitchen.

"I think I scared him," Tealy stated. "I had a moment when I got back from being at on the island with you and mom. I lost it, and in the middle of my meltdown, I said a few things I know I didn't mean. At least I hope I didn't."

"Are you leaving him?" CeCe interjected.

"No. Never. I couldn't do that. I was just overwhelmed," Tealy admitted. "Anyway, Grant's really stepping it up around here for me. I do love how he's helping more with the kids. I guess I didn't realize how badly I do need a hand with them sometimes."

"Well yeah, you're not Wonder Woman!" CeCe told her, seriously, but she did smile at her word choice.

"We're fine. I'm fine. Don't say anything to mom, okay?" Tealy wanted that reassurance. The last thing she needed was Poppy worried about her marriage crumbling. She was still dealing with the fallout of her own.

"Not a word from me," CeCe said, but she envied her sister at the moment because their mother would not meddle in her personal life, as she just had in hers.

"Do you want to sit down? Have a glass of wine or something?" Tealy offered.

"No, I want to go home. I have to work early tomorrow. But, thank you for the offer — and especially for not wrecking my new SUV once you left the ferry." Tealy rolled her eyes and CeCe laughed out loud.

"Thank you for ensuring that I got back home to my family when they needed me," Tealy told her big sister. She was genuinely grateful to borrow CeCe's vehicle. "I hope you and mom enjoyed your time together after I left." There it was. It was always about jealously between sisters.

"We did actually," CeCe sort of lied. Being confronted about having an affair was not exactly a grand time.

"Good. Take a look at your calendar and we'll go back again soon," Tealy suggested.

"Sure. I'll let you know," CeCe didn't seem interested. Tealy wasn't surprised. Time off in a career like hers was a rarity, or at least she claimed it was. And it had almost seemed as if that's the way CeCe preferred it.

✕ ✕ ✕

When CeCe backed out of the driveway of her sister's half a million dollar two-story home, she spoke aloud to herself. "Appreciate what you have, little sister. I blew my chance." *Had she really passed up a life that she claimed not to want?* A marriage and children were never of interest, or included in CeCe's plan. She was a career woman, through and through. Until she met Stu Brentwood. Until he had proposed marriage to her, despite how they initially had an agreement. *Had he really wanted to marry her first and foremost in his heart?* CeCe was thinking crazy. She was out of routine. She needed to sleep in her own bed tonight, and resume her life behind the camera tomorrow. She was the one who gave Stu the final push into her best friend's arms. He was going to be elected Mayor of Boston. CeCe wasn't cut out for that kind of lifestyle. She was no good when all eyes were on her. The spotlight wasn't for her. She was made for behind the scenes. CeCe knew it, and so did Stu. That was ultimately why he chose to make another woman his wife. Someone who fit the part for the life he dreamed of living.

Cece's phone rang just as she rolled backwards off the curb of Tealy's driveway. She looked down at the home screen, face up and lit up, on the passenger seat. The picture staring back at her was of Jen in her wedding dress, and CeCe was hugging her neck. *Friends. Best friends.* CeCe would always carry guilt for being with Stu — and never choosing to give him up. Not even for the sake of her best friend's happiness. But it wouldn't stop CeCe from being with him. He was hers first. Jen was calling now. For a moment, CeCe considered letting the voicemail pick up.

"Hey married lady!" CeCe answered the call.

"It's going to blow," Jen's voice spoke on the other end.

"What's going to blow? What are you talking about? If you're messing with me again, I'll have you know I just spent two days on an island with my mother so I'm all out of sarcasm." CeCe giggled, but there was no response on the other end of the phone. "Jen? Are you still there?"

"I'm sure I was the butt of your jokes, you know the ones between the two of you when you were lying naked in each other's arms." *Oh my God. She knows.* "Don't you know me at all, C? I always get the last word, the last laugh. So I'll say it again, it's going to blow."

CeCe was stunned to silence. *What the hell was she to say to that? Jen knew about her and Stu. And she had resorted to drastic measures. But how? Who was going to suffer? And what was going to blow?*

CeCe threw her gear into drive and sped down the roadway, leading out of Tealy's subdivision. "I'm on my way to see you right now. Stay put!" CeCe assumed she was at home. At her newly built house that she planned to share with Stu for the rest of their lives.

"You're out of time. You can't fix this. And you can't have him anymore." Jen ended the call. CeCe drove too fast as she debated whether or not to call Jen back, or to get Stu on the phone now. She chose Stu. *Hadn't she always?*

His cell phone rang too many times.

"Pick up, Stu!" CeCe pounded her phoneless hand on the steering wheel before she gripped it again to make a turn that would lead her to downtown Boston — to Stu's office. She would take a chance to find him there. They needed to fix this. End this. *Something!*

The fact was, she had just missed him. Five minutes ago, he was walking to his car from his high rise office building. His wife had sent him a text message. *Leave now. I need you.* He rushed out. He was going home first, as he assumed that's where Jen had texted him from. He worried when she didn't respond to his messages, or his attempt to call her back. He took the bait, he left. He unlocked his car, and he rushed to sit behind the wheel, and turned the key into the ignition. And that's when his car exploded into an instantaneous fireball in the middle of the parking garage. His dearly beloved wife had timed his demise perfectly, just as she had planned it for a very long time. *It's going to blow.* It certainly did.

Chapter fifteen

Two-inch black heels held up her five-foot-nine frame. She wore a just-above-the-knee, straight black dress with three quarter-length sleeves. It was all over. The funeral visitation. The memorial service to remember and honor his life. The burial of his remains in the City of Boston cemetery. There was no casket, no body. There was nothing left to view. He left this world in such a morbidly tragic manner. And all that was left of him was dust in an urn.

CeCe was able to attend the funeral of the man she loved. The accident was under investigation. It would just be a matter of time before phone records were traced to her. She would be labeled as a mistress. Her name would be dragged through the press, and the rumor mill. CeCe's image would be tarnished for awhile. But at least she wasn't a murderer. Her best friend and wife of the murder victim was arrested immediately following her husband's funeral. CeCe avoided the sudden scene on the cemetery grounds, where the urn of ashes was to be buried. She just kept walking to her vehicle as the police detectives were cuffing her best friend at the site where her husband was said to rest in peace. It was only a matter of time before they caught her, CeCe had warned Jen.

At the explosion site, CeCe's worst nightmare came true. She had known before she arrived on the emergent scene. She could feel it. Their connection had ceased. Stu was gone. And her best friend was to blame. His new wife had killed him. What CeCe and Stu had done together, for years, had caught up with them in the worst way.

CeCe took the elevator up to the fifth floor. It was four-thirty in the afternoon. As far back as she could remember, her father's patient appointments ended at four-thirty. That varied if he had an emergency, or was in the operating room. Today, she knew, he was at the office.

Reed's secretary waved at CeCe as she was leaving for the day. "Your dad is here. Go on in," she told CeCe as she caught the same elevator.

CeCe opened his office door without knocking. Her father was sitting in front of his laptop. His glasses were low on his nose. He was starting to look like a grandpa, CeCe suddenly thought. The man she always saw as youthful, strong, and invincible was aging. CeCe couldn't help but think the loss of two loves in his life had everything to do with that.

"Hey baby girl," Reed removed his reading glasses and stood up. CeCe never said a word in response as her steps quickened to get to him. He was waiting with open arms.

CeCe sobbed on the shoulder of his long sleeve white dress shirt. "I can't do this, daddy," he heard her say. "How am I going to survive without him?"

Reed knew of his daughter's relationship with Stu Brentwood. She had come to him a year ago when Jen came into Stu's life — and she became the other woman. CeCe knew her father would understand because she was the only person in his life who had known about his affair.

It happened when CeCe was sixteen. She was driving alone through downtown Boston. It was almost her ten o'clock curfew. She passed her father's office on her way home. She saw his vehicle parked outside. The brake lights were lit. He was behind the wheel, and when he started to drive off, CeCe followed him. She initially thought he was going home. But her father made other turns, a route that peaked CeCe's curiosity. He drove to the apartments on the east side of town. CeCe started to feel uneasy about what was happening. She followed at least two car lengths behind him, keeping her distance to be less obvious.

Across the street from the apartment complex, CeCe parked and shut off the engine. She sat inside of her dark car, the brand new BMW convertible that her father had just bought for her sweet sixteenth. She watched from under the street light as her father got out of his SUV, and he wasn't alone. A petite blonde woman, that was all CeCe could distinguish in the dark, exited the passenger side of her father's vehicle. He was at her side when her feet stepped off the running board and hit the ground. He pulled her close. And CeCe witnesses them in a passionate lip lock. Her heart sunk. She was going to be sick. She'd felt like throwing up on her lap, right there on the leather interior. Instead, hot tears sprung to her eyes.

CeCe reacted immediately. She opened her car door, and was on foot, on an angry mission to confront her father right then and there.

"How could you!" she recalled, screaming to the point of reaching hysterics. The woman immediately looked to Reed for direction. He sent her inside, where CeCe assumed she lived. And in that dark parking lot, Reed asked his daughter to get into his vehicle with him. She balked. He persisted. And then she did as her father ordered.

CeCe could still remember all that was said between them on that night.

You can't tell your mother. It will crush her. I love her. I need her in my life. I'm serious, C. I can't live without her. We have to keep our family together. Stay quiet. There are things you won't under-stand, but someday you will. What you saw is my business, not yours.

CeCe had cried. *I can't lie to mom. I'll be no better than you are, if I keep your secret.*

But she nonetheless had kept her father's secret for another fifteen years. She may not have entirely understood his actions, his justification, then. But she did now. She had lived that kind of life. She was sucked in, intoxicated, drugged. Stu Brentwood was her addiction.

In her father's arms now, CeCe felt connected to him in a way that had multiplied immeasurably. He knew how she felt. He too had been thrown onto the merciless battleground of grief. *Was it karma? One hell of a payback?* It didn't even matter. Pain was pain.

"Jen was arrested, just now at the cemetery," CeCe told her father, as she used her fingers to wipe away the tears on her face. He still had one arm around her while she spoke.

"You knew that was coming," Reed stated, as a matter of fact. "I can't believe she went to those lengths. She killed him. My God, none of us are what we seem, are we?" And that was a fact. For two decades, Reed Brennan had lived a double life. The upstanding oral surgeon, a family man with values. And now his daughter would be exposed as being no better than him. She was having an affair with her best friend's husband. She stood up for them as the maid of honor at their wedding in the park just barely one week ago.

"I've lost so much," CeCe said, referring to her torn apart life at the moment.

"You and me both, kiddo," Reed spoke solemnly.

"I'm sorry, dad. I'm being insensitive. I know you get this, more than anyone. I just wish you could tell me it will get better. I can't fathom feeling anything else but lost and empty."

"Keep busy. Throw yourself into your work." *As if CeCe was unfamiliar with that.* "That's the best advice I can give you," Reed gently touched his daughter's cheek.

"Yeah? And how's that working for you?" CeCe asked him.

"Not so good," he sighed.

✗ ✗ ✗

Poppy now had a new deadbolt on the cottage door —which she had never concerned herself with locking before— as well as first-time locks on all of the windows. *It was just a precaution,* she told herself. *Dudley was harmless.*

It had been three days since she saw him last. Poppy spent her time browsing the shops on island, and walking the beach late in the afternoon when the air temperature was its warmest. She bundled in layers to tolerate the forty-something degree wind chill near the water, but her feet were still bare. The sand through her toes was the most remedial feeling.

She also found herself on the floor at the bottom of the hall closet, at least once a day. She continued to sort through all of the old photographs. The keep, frame later, pile of hers had grown. She thought about calling Van again, just to pick his brain about her mother some more. *What else had she not known about Julie Blare?*

Poppy's isolation at the cottage had kept her completely out of the loop. No television and rare use of the internet on her phone had prevented her from hearing the news reports about the explosive murder in Boston. And no one from home had called her.

Reed knew better. He would be accused of passing on the cheat gene through his corrupt DNA.

CeCe didn't want her mother coming to her rescue, as she knew she would have been there for the funeral.

Tealy was boiling mad. She had, once again, been the last to know. She, out of spite, threatened to tell their mother. CeCe warned her she would never speak to her again if she did. She would cut her out of her life completely— her rug rats too. It took three days before Tealy couldn't take it anymore. Their mother needed to know.

Poppy was in the kitchen, debating on making a trip to the market again. She was getting quite used to living off of seafood and fresh vegetables. And she was almost out of wine again. Her phone rang, as she spotted it on the counter with her car keys. *She really should check her messages more,* she thought. But that was the beauty of isolation. She didn't have to stay in touch with anyone.

"Hi sweetie," Poppy referred to Tealy on the opposite end of the phone.

"I take it all of your connections to the outside world are still shut down," Tealy spoke sarcastically. *That girl and her sass.* Both of Poppy's girls were knee deep in sarcasm.

"Yes, purposefully," Poppy replied. "I hope you're calling just to chat, but something tells me there's a tidbit of information that you want me to know about."

"It's more than a tidbit, mother," Tealy stated. "Your other daughter is a fucking mess, and the current state of her life reflects that!"

Poppy wondered if Tealy knew. *Stu Brentwood was CeCe's lover.* She kept quiet, and waited for Tealy to tell her. The last thing Poppy wanted was to reveal a secret that would put her daughters even more at odds than they often were.

"Stu Brentwood," Tealy began, and Poppy thought, *ah yes, here we go...* "is dead."

"What?" Poppy spoke with immediate alarm in her voice. *Dead? CeCe must be devastated. And Jen too. Why in the hell was a thirty-something man DEAD?*

"He was murdered. A car bomb in a parking garage. And here's the kicker, mother... the news played this out for me, because my own sister is a complete stranger to me! Yeah, that's right. I had to find out from the Channel 5 anchor that Stu Brennan's wife had him killed because she was a woman scorned — and the culprit screwing her husband was none other than my big sister!"

"Oh my God? Jen? Jen killed him? This is ludicrous!" Poppy was pacing in her small kitchen, but she probably should have just sat down. This felt like too much for her to handle. She was sick and tired of juggling the shock and the hurt.

"You knew didn't you?" Tealy called out her mother at the most inappropriate time. "You were aware of the affair."

"I just found out when the two of you were on island, but that is beside the point!" Poppy scolded her youngest daughter. "When did this happen? I have to get home. CeCe must be beside herself! Dear God, the funeral, Jen will go to jail—"

"We're way ahead of you with that," Tealy interjected.

"What? When did this happen?" Poppy pressed her.

"Three days ago. Stu is dead and buried, well what's left of him. And Jen was arrested, of all places, at the cemetery!"

Poppy covered her mouth with her hand. Her daughter's reputation would be trashed. Just like Reed's. Poppy certainly knew what it felt like to be on the receiving end of the ongoing gossip and the stares. And *she* was the innocent victim.

"No one contacted me," Poppy said, sadly.

"CeCe warned me not to. She didn't want you to have to come home. I think she's leaning on dad quite a bit, or at least that's my guess."

"Of course," Poppy replied. But little did Poppy know the full extent of Reed's bond with their oldest daughter.

"I'm sorry if you're hurt, mom. I couldn't take it anymore. I had to tell you." Tealy actually sounded sincere.

"I'm fine. Just very worried about your sister, and I'm sure Jen's parents are devastated. Listen Tealy, I have to go. I should at least make some phone calls if I'm not going to return home."

Tealy knew her mother meant she was going to immediately end their call so she could reach out to CeCe. "Tell my sister to have a nice life…or at least what's left of it."

"Dammit Tealy! Shut up. She's in pain. She needs us." Poppy could easily reach her wits end with her daughters and their lack of closeness.

"I just meant that she told me she would be out of my life, and my kids' lives, if I were to tell you this before she was ready," Tealy defended herself.

"Grow up, Tealy. She didn't mean it. We are family, like it or not we will always be in each other's lives." Poppy had enough. She ended that call first.

Chapter sixteen

CeCe stared out of the window of her penthouse, overlooking Pier 4. It was luxury living, that's what Stu had always told her. That building was Boston's first-service residential. If she wanted, CeCe could have taken advantage of the chef services, the in-home botanical care, and the door to door messenger. The only amenity that CeCe relished was the fitness studio. She had a gym in her building that she frequented daily. She used to tease Stu that she was going to get a dog just to take part in the pet-friendly environment. There was a dog spa on the premises for pets to be pampered. There was an on-site dog washing room, she giggled when they had walked by it together one day, and Stu had said, *I'll get you a dog, I'll buy you whatever you want. Just marry me.*

She blinked back the tears. That was all he wanted, and CeCe had not given in. She was the one who pushed him into *Jen's life, Jen's arms, Jen's bed.* If only CeCe had been able to recognize how much her father had influenced her life, after that one night when she was sixteen years old, and forced to grow up. A small part of CeCe had actually been relieved when the truth came out, more than a decade later. *At least she no longer had to lie to her mother.* Even still, if Poppy were to ever find out, she would disown her oldest daughter. CeCe had absolutely no doubt.

She hadn't slept much at all since the night Stu died. She was used to him being there. They were going to make their lives together work, he had promised her. He would still spend some nights with her, in the bed at the penthouse that had become *theirs.* There was an indent on the mattress where his body had left a curve. CeCe couldn't bear to look at it now, or to be in that bed without him. She took the couch last night, and the previous nights, since he was gone.

Standing barefoot on the hardwood flooring of her penthouse, CeCe wore nothing but a long-sleeved button down powder blue shirt that Stu had left behind. Her long dark hair was up in a knot on top of her head. She wore no makeup. She needed to take a shower, brush her teeth, and eat, or at least drink, something. Depriving her body of what it needed was CeCe's way of punishing herself. And she knew it had to stop. She just didn't know how to stop herself. The pain was getting the best of her.

The ringtone of her phone startled her in that spacious, quiet penthouse. CeCe would look to see who was calling, but if it wasn't her boss or her father, she wouldn't answer.

She hadn't thought about it being her mother.

"Hello?" CeCe realized the sadness and the pain in her voice would give her away, if her mother had not already known. *Damn you, Tealy,* if Poppy knew.

"Honey…" The emotion in Poppy's voice said it all. *She knew.*

"Mom…" CeCe choked on a sob, and then completely broke down.

"You should have called me. I would have come. You know that. This is too much for you to handle alone. Let me be your strength." Poppy rambled as CeCe cried. She wasn't even sure if she could hear her.

"I can't believe it, mom. She killed him. She wanted him to pay, but you know what? He's dead, and as absurd as this is going to sound, he's feeling nothing right now. She went about it all wrong! She didn't cause him pain. She ended his pain. He doesn't have to feel what I feel. Lost and lonely and desperate to know if this is how I am always going to be. I'm envious of Stu because he doesn't have to feel like this!" CeCe continued to cry, and the more Poppy listened to her speak, the more frightened for her daughter she became.

"Maybe that's what Jen wanted," Poppy spoke. She sounded strong, but she was reeling for her daughter's pain. "Look, I adored that girl. I never in my wildest dreams ever would have pegged her as capable of murder. But I've been where she was when she found out, however she found out, about you and her husband. I'm telling you, if your father's *other woman* had not already been in a coffin, I could have easily lost it to the point of putting her in one!"

CeCe was stunned to silence for a moment. "So instead of wanting me dead, Jen wanted me to suffer like I am now — mourning Stu and what we had together?"

"Yes, that's exactly how she probably feels. Honey, I am not taking sides here. I'm just pointing out that Jen wanted you to pay dearly. And I know you are, but you cannot let her win. She ruined her life. That doesn't mean you have to allow yours to be as good as nothing as if you were rotting away in a prison cell, too."

"I needed this from you, mom. I just didn't know how to reach out and tell you without drudging up your pain from dad that's still so raw, too." CeCe sniffed into the phone and then used the floppy sleeve of Stu's shirt to wipe her nose.

"I will catch the next ferry off the island," Poppy stated.

"No. Please. I need some time. I don't know, a few days or maybe a week. I have no idea what I'm going to do about work yet, but I want to come see you again. I liked it there. Is it healing you, mom? I want it to do that for me." CeCe started to cry again.

"I will be here when you are ready," Poppy began. "Just promise me one thing. Promise me that your will never lose sight of how much your life matters. That man, of your inner-most beliefs, may have hung the moon and every twinkling star, but he was just a man. You will love again, my darling little girl." Poppy wanted to take her own advice to heart. She had faith, and she did want to find love again. She may have been more than a half a century old, but she was too young to grow old alone. She just needed to get over Reed first. He was her knight and shining armor — who let her down.

"Mom, thank you. I mean it, thank you for not hating me, and not taking Jen's side. I know you can relate to her pain more than anyone else. I am the cause of this tragedy," CeCe choked back her tears this time.

"It wasn't you alone," Poppy stated. "All three of you played with fire. Don't you take all of the blame. Get out of that penthouse. Go to work. You've always been good at allowing your career to consume you."

"That was dad's advice, too," CeCe told her mother, but instantly wondered if she shouldn't have spoken it.

"He would know," Poppy stated, and then ended the call just before she broke down on the kitchen floor of the cottage. Her daughter's pain was most definitely her pain, as well. But this. This hit a little too close to Poppy's already broken, bleeding, betrayed heart.

#️⃣

Poppy left the cottage and went for a drive. She went to the market for wine. From her childhood she had vivid memories of her grandmother and her mother having a glass of wine. Neither one of them, from what Poppy recalled, drank excessively. They just drank when necessary. When life needed to be escaped for a little while.

She wore flared faded denim with a winter white turtle neck, which offered just enough warmth for another cloudy, chilly November day on island. Her feet were chilled in her flip flops, but Poppy preferred it that way. Her toes were polished cherry red still. It was the only nail polish she had packed. Maybe she would buy one or two other colors sometime when she was out shopping.

Poppy was beginning to recognize the staff at the market, and they her. She had just placed some eggs into her cart, beside three bottles of white wine and fresh swordfish, when Poppy looked up to find another grocery cart nose to nose with hers.

"Hello Dudley," she spoke first. Her voice was strong and confident, because that's who she was. It was time that Poppy owned her life. Being alone at the cottage had already taught her that. What was happening to her daughter right now had blatantly reminded Poppy the importance of being a woman who could stand on her own two feet — even when she was hurting inside.

Dudley wore a gray jacket that she had seen once before. He had on different pants, these were cargo khakis, Poppy noticed. He also wore a new colored ball cap. Gray, to match his jacket. Like her, he still chose to wear flip flops.

"Hi Poppy. Time to stock up, again," he teased, looking at more wine in her grocery cart.

"Yep," she smiled. "So, how are you holding up?"

"Good, actually. My sons were home for a few days." *Ah, that explained his absence.*

"That's great," Poppy offered. She wondered what his boys were like. *Had they missed their mother? Were they close with their father all of their lives, or especially now?*

"Listen, this probably isn't the time or place, but I just want to say I'm sorry that I overstepped. Grief sucks. I'm lonely. I just enjoy being with you, talking, I mean. I would like to be friends."

Poppy looked around as if someone would overhear their conversation. She really didn't care. No one knew her personally on island anyway. "Friends. I'd like that," she smiled. She still had her guard up, because she really did not know Dudley Connors at all. But she also sympathized with him. He was in pain. No one was themselves when they were suffering. Poppy thought of Jen, locked behind the bars of a jail cell. She didn't deserve that either.

"I have a suggestion," Dudley spoke again. "Take your eggs and whatever else back to the cottage to be refrigerated, and then meet me in an hour or so at Lookout Tavern. You have to eat dinner, right? So do I, and I don't know about you but for me eating alone isn't any fun."

Poppy smiled again. *Should she? Or shouldn't she?*

Did she have to remind herself that she summoned a locksmith not too long ago because she feared what this man might do if he wanted to see her? There was absolutely no sign of *that Dudley* who she had felt uncertain to be alone with. So Poppy said yes to dinner. Dinner in a public place, to where they would drive separate cars. *What was the harm?*

Chapter seventeen

Poppy returned to downtown and was at Lookout Tavern an hour and fifteen minutes later. She never bothered to change her clothes. The pub wasn't a fancy environment, and she wasn't out to impress Dudley. This wasn't a date. He said so himself, *they were friends.* She did curl her hair and apply some eye makeup and lipstick just to feel refreshed.

She arrived first and went inside. The hostess offered her a table for one, and Poppy replied that she was waiting on someone, but would like to be seated and order a glass of white wine. She never had the chance to open a bottle she bought at the market.

Poppy was perched on a chair at a high table in the corner. She sipped her wine and looked around a bit. She liked that place. The lunch menu had been delicious when she was there with her girls, and now she was starved for almost anything for dinner there. She prepared to ask for a menu if the waitress came by again while she waited for Dudley. She really had no idea what kind of person he was, she thought, as she sipped her wine. She knew he was dependable in his job, because he had readied the cottage for her in a moment's notice. She knew he loved his late wife, and obviously cherished his boys. But was he an on-time kind of guy? Did he fill up his gas tank when it was half empty or wait until the car was slated for its last mile? Poppy was an error on the side of caution person. Reed was not. He took risks. Obviously. But, sadly now, that had been one of the things she loved most about him.

"Excuse me?" Poppy heard a male voice, as she looked up from her wine. "Is that seat taken?" It was Dudley. Same clothes and cap as before. He had the same idea as she did. Not a date. Just dinner between friends.

"Yes, actually, I'm waiting for my friend," Poppy teased.

Dudley laughed. "Well I hope for that to be me." He sat on that vacant high chair, opposite of hers.

Casual and easy conversation took place between them before Dudley ordered a longneck and a crab burger. The idea of a crab cake between a bun sounded unique and delicious to Poppy, but she opted for the blackened Mahi Mahi.

When their waitress stopped by the table to tell them that their dinner would be out shortly, Poppy requested a second glass of wine when Dudley asked for another beer. Poppy then excused herself to use the ladies room. She was having a nice time with him. She laughed at herself for thinking he was crazed and possibly dangerous.

On her way to the restroom, Poppy noticed a man walking toward her. It was a busy restaurant during the dinner hour. It was loud in there, too, just as it had been during lunch with her daughters. The man made direct eye contact with her. He was Poppy's age bracket. His short hair was almost all gray. Men could pull off the distinguished look with graying hair, most women could not. Poppy, at least, didn't want to be one of them.

The man was in her way, directly in front of her. Poppy stopped. He did too. "This is going to sound strange, because I remember you, and you probably do not have a clue who I am," he began, and there was something very familiar about his mouth. Those full lips on a round, tanned face with light blue eyes. Poppy couldn't believe it. Her next thought brought her back in time, on the fishing dock just off the beach. He kissed her. Her first kiss. One she had never forgotten. It was like melting butter on her tongue. *Kirk…what was his last name? Kirk! Holy smokes, forty-one years later…*

"Nineteen seventy-six. The cottages on the beach. Frisbee. Fishing. And maybe a kiss under the moonlight…" *He clearly still hadn't forgotten either.* "You're Poppy Blare, aren't you?"

"Brennan," she corrected, but wondered why that was necessary.

"I knew it!" he smiled. "You really haven't changed a bit."

"Oh please, I was twelve!" she laughed. "Kirk, right? Forgive me, but your last name escapes me." He was taller, of course he would be taller than he was when he was fourteen. He was thicker. His chest. His arms. His waistline. Poppy momentarily recalled the abs that boy used to have. That boy was now a man.

"Lane. I heard you were on island, actually. So I may have had the upper hand, knowing I could possibly run into the beautiful brunette from one of my best summers as a teenager," Kirk Lane paused. "I never had the chance to tell you how sorry I was about what happened."

"Thank you," Poppy nodded. He didn't need to say *what happened to her brother*. She knew he was aware. There was an all too familiar, sympathetic look in his eyes. It was such a sad story for anyone to hear about.

"So are you back on island for awhile?" Kirk asked her, and she wanted to stand there and talk to him — but her bladder was threatening to explode, and Dudley was waiting. Their dinner plates probably had arrived at the table by now.

"Yes, I think so." She wanted to ask him if he lived on island, if he had ever left? But again, she had to go. In more ways than one.

"I'll be quick," Kirk said, and it was as if he read her mind. "I'm the chief of the Oak Bluffs Police Department." Kirk unzipped his jacket to reveal a silver, metal, oval shaped law badge hanging off of the belt weaved through the loops of his denim. "I saw you dining with a man over there in the corner." He paused before he spoke again. "Be careful, Poppy."

"Excuse me?" she purposely turned her head and stretched her neck to see if she could spot Dudley waiting alone at their table. There were too many heads in the crowded restaurant.

"Dudley Connors, right?"

She nodded. And she tried not to feel panicked.

"He's a loner. We watch him now and then," Kirk offered.

"Is he a criminal?" Poppy blurted out.

"He's looking. Always looking for something, or someone. It's suspicious behavior in my book. I don't know how well you know him, but I wanted to alert you to just watch your back. Keep your guard up. Call me, if you feel uneasy. You know my number," he stated with a lopsided grin. *Dial 911, and ask for Kirk Lane,* Poppy thought, and she wanted to smile but she was scared of what the Oak Bluffs Chief of Police was telling her.

"I just feel for him," Poppy admitted. "I consider him a friend." Poppy thought of sleeping with him. Hot sex on the floor of her cottage. All friendship boundaries had definitely been blown past that night.

"Friends are good to have. Just pick the right ones," Kirk advised her.

"You're scaring me, and now I have to get back to my table with him and eat dinner," Poppy all but scolded him—this man, this blast from her past.

"He could be harmless," Kirk offered, and Poppy recalled also using that very same adjective regarding Dudley.

"I know, I know, so I'll just keep my guard up," she reiterated. "I do feel sorry for him. He just lost his wife, and all."

Kirk frowned. This was a red flag. He stepped closer to Poppy, as if to secure some sort of private exchange, and he lowered his voice as he spoke, "his wife died three years ago."

Chapter eighteen

Poppy's heart rate quickened. She thought for sure she was going to either faint or lose control of her bladder right there.

"I need to leave here," she whispered to him. "My purse, with my car keys and my phone, is back at the table where I left Dudley."

"Don't leave. And most important, don't panic," Kirk told her in what Poppy believed was his Chief of Police voice. "Go where you were headed, to the restroom, and return to your table. Eat dinner, and then tell him you need to get home. You're tired. You have a headache. You know, say what you women say," he smiled, and Poppy tried to relax. "I will be here watching you, and I'll follow you out of here, too. Stay calm. I've got your back, Poppy."

She inhaled a deep breath. "Okay, I can do that. Thank you." She didn't know if she should have thanked him yet. This seemed to be far from over. For now, she just wanted *the chief* to see to it that she got back to the cottage alone, where she could deadbolt the door.

⚡⚡⚡

Poppy stood in front of the sink in the restroom. She was alone in there. She faced the mirror. That woman in the reflection had been through some real shit in her life. But she was stronger because of all of it. Poppy truly believed that. She saw pain in her eyes. The pain from being back on the island, where the memories of Bobby continued to wash in, like the ocean waves rushing onto the beach. The pain from Reed's betrayal. And now, the fear of being hurt again. *What did Dudley want from her?* Whatever he was after, Poppy was going to stay one step ahead of him now.

She returned to their table to find him gone. The table was empty. Her wine glass and his beer bottle were both gone. It looked as if no dinner plates had ever arrived. Poppy quickly glanced at her chair to find that her purse was still there, as she left it. She looked around, but she didn't see Dudley. Had he stepped away from the table, too? *To the bar? The restroom?*

Their same waitress from earlier approached her, and Poppy spoke first. "The man I was with —gray baseball cap— have you seen him?"

"He cancelled your dinner order, paid for your drinks, and left. I think he saw you talking to that other guy, near the restrooms. He seemed upset." That was a lot of information for the waitress to offer. Poppy nodded and walked away. She felt frazzled as she rushed out of the restaurant to her car. It was well-lit in the parking lot and busy with people coming and going. Poppy reminded herself that she was safe as she unlocked her car, got inside behind the wheel, and locked it again.

＃ ＃ ＃

Poppy turned every single light on inside of the cottage when she got there. She had feared Dudley might be inside, somewhere. It was a crazy notion. She had the deadbolt changed, his existing key would not fit the lock. The worst part of this was they were enjoying each other's company again. Tonight had been simple and honest, or so she had thought. *Dudley's wife hadn't just died? Kirk said the police have been watching him because of implied strange behavior.* Dudley lied to her, manipulated her. She slept with him for chrissakes. *Big mistake, Poppy.*

She stood in the middle of the living room for a moment. Wine. She needed wine to calm her nerves. She took the steps toward the kitchen just as her cell phone in her hand rang. She jumped and let out a sudden squeal. *Calm down, Poppy.*

The number had been programmed in her phone as *cottage caretaker.* She had never changed it to Dudley Connors. In any case, *he* was calling her.

Poppy inhaled a deep breath before she answered. "Dudley? What's going on? You ditched me before dinner." She purposely played it cool.

"Are you upset with me?" his voice sounded strange. Creepy again. Poppy imagined one of those horror movie scenes, when the wacko was locked in a secret room somewhere with photographs of his prey plastered all over the wall. *Was she Dudley's victim? Was he obsessed with having her? Would he kill her?* That was absurd.

"No, but I'm not happy that I didn't get to eat some really good food tonight. Why did you leave without saying a word?" Poppy was trying her to best to be nonchalant.

"You were gone a really long time. I saw you talking to someone." *Had Dudley known the chief of police?* "It's silly of me, I know, but I felt jealous."

Poppy needed to be careful with that comment from him. Dudley was acting as if he owned her, which justified her recent thought of him being obsessed with her. "Jealous? Oh, come on, that's crazy!" *Maybe crazy wasn't the most fitting word choice.* "Dudley, we talked about this. We are friends."

"Friends," he repeated. "Right. I shouldn't have left the restaurant the way I did. I'm sorry."

"You're fine," she was quick to respond.

"Can I come over for a drink?" he asked, and her eyes widened, as she stood all by herself in the middle of the cottage's kitchen.

"No!" she may have been too quick to shut him down. "I mean, I have a headache, probably because I have not eaten anything yet. I should munch on a little something, and then go to bed."

"Some other time?" he asked her.

"Sure," she responded. "Good night, Dudley." She abruptly ended the call.

Chapter nineteen

Poppy was not sure how, but she managed to get a restful night's sleep. She awoke curled up on the white suede sofa with a stemless glass placed near the edge of the wagon wheel table in front of her. Left, in that glass, was one swallow of white wine.

She made her way to the kitchen and ate a piece of toast, generously buttered. Then she stripped her clothes off and took a long, hot shower. She thought of her daughters, especially CeCe who was going through pure hell right now. And then Reed crossed her mind. At least he would be good for something these days. He could talk to their daughter, and help her through a familiar pain. Poppy tried not to think of him as she blow dried her hair, but her thoughts inevitably shifted to Dudley. She was not going to live in fear. She was not going to let him, or anyone else, keep her from peacefully being on that island. Dudley had lied to her about his wife's death. Poppy was sick and tired of being lied to, played for a fool. She got dressed in black leggings, a charcoal gray hoodie, and her flip flops. The sun was shining for the first time in days. She was going to take a morning walk on the beach.

With the wind at her back, she walked to the three-mile marker before she turned around to head back. The cold air cut right through her, and she immediately knew it was going to be unpleasant to walk back. She wished she had worn another layer underneath her sweatshirt. But she would survive. One bare foot in front of the other in the sand. That mirrored her life more than Poppy realized. The walk had not always been pleasant, but she had persevered.

She was chilled to the bone, as her hands were placed in the front pocket of her sweatshirt and her hood was up. She pulled the drawstrings and tied her hood in place a few miles back to keep it from blowing off of her head. Before she reached the cottage, she glanced over at the fishing dock. It was such a staple to her. There were good memories made on that dock. She tried to act at ease and keep walking. She tried not to focus on what she saw there again. But he had already spotted her looking. Poppy was certain he had been staring and waiting for her to see him. *Had he also been there when she left to walk the beach earlier?*

Poppy was half-tempted to keep walking, to make her way up through the sand to the boardwalk, and onto the porch. She wished to be on the other side of that deadbolt on the cottage door. But no, she was not going to run from this. It was still possible that Dudley was harmless, that he only wanted her attention. But, Poppy was done. She didn't need a friend on the island. That was the very last thing she came there for. And it was time to speak her mind.

"Hi there," she said to him, as she removed her hood and stepped onto the fishing dock.

"Good morning, beautiful," Dudley replied, and Poppy awkwardly looked down at her feet.

"It's rather chilly to just be sitting out here, don't you think? I've been walking for miles and still can't seem to warm up," Poppy noted.

"This is where to find me in any kind of weather. I come here to think. This was my spot long before you arrived on island. Just what if it's meant to be though? Us, as a significant part of each other's lives. I know we agreed to rewind this relationship and begin again as friends, but I'm going to just put this out there for you to think about. I am falling in love with you." Poppy froze. She didn't want this, nor had she expected to hear those words from him so soon. Or ever. "My wife would want me to move on." *Yes, his wife. And how long had she been gone? Just weeks? Or three years? Liar.*

"Dudley, listen… I have a lot going on in my life. I came here for peace and isolation. I need space. What happened between us, happened. We can't be together like that again. I hope you'll understand." Poppy held her breath and she watched him stumble to his feet.

"I can give you space," he started to say.

"No, you can't. You're always here, just feet from my home. You were in the restaurant I chose to dine at with my girls. You were in the grocery store when I was. I can't help it, but I feel like you are watching me, and following me. This island is not that big, but it is big enough for us to keep our distance from each other. Namely, you from me. Stay away from me. I do not want you in my life. I feel terrible if I led you on in any way. I had too much to drink. I was lonely. Being together was a mistake." Poppy held nothing back.

Dudley's face fell. He just stood there with the look of a lost child. "You can't mean that," she heard him say in what was barely a whisper. She watched his lip quiver. *My God, this man was unstable. How had she not seen this before? It was as if he was bipolar, mentally ill. That had to be the only explanation.* "I just told you that I am falling in love with you. This can work! We connected! I haven't been able to find that with anyone in a very long time!" Dudley was yelling and his entire body shook. It was cold out there on the water, but he was also reacting to her with shock and anger. Poppy obviously had not told him what he wanted to hear. He stomped his foot down with so much force on the wooden dock that two of the boards split and completely broke through. The wooden dock was old and weathered, it could have been brittle in spots. Poppy was dumbfounded. His level of anger was frightening. Poppy's first and only reaction was to begin to back away from him, but he charged her. She moved, instantly and quickly, but when she spun her body around, she lost her balance and Dudley grabbed ahold of her by the throat. He tightened both of his hands around her airway. She could not breathe at all. She batted her arms in a vicious attempt to strike his face. He was much stronger than she was. His eyes, only inches from hers, were distant and angry. He was choking the life out of her. But she wasn't giving up. She was not going down without a fight. She brought her knee up as fast and with as much force as she could possibly muster, and she rammed it into his groin. Dudley doubled over. His hands were finally freed from her neck. Poppy coughed, and sucked in as much air as she could at once. She felt light-headed. She stumbled backwards. And then she lost her balance and fell in between the broken slabs of wood on the dock, and into the water. It was freezing and instantly a frigid shock to her body. She was an experienced swimmer, but she would have to go all the way under the water, beneath the dock, to get away from him. Pulling herself up through the broken slabs of wood on the dock was not an option. As she willed herself to brave the conditions, to beat the hypothermia that threatened to kill her right then and there, Poppy looked up through the dock to find Dudley staring down at her. He reached for the hood of her sweatshirt, and for a moment Poppy believed he was going to pull her up, and help her out of the water. Instead, she saw the very same look in his eyes that terrified her before. He forced her under the water and held her there. Like the memory of almost every child in a swimming pool, Poppy felt on the receiving end of being dunked. But this was no game. This was real life. This was beyond serious and dangerous. Dudley, a man scorned, or so he had wrongly believed, was going to drown her.

Poppy fought him. She forced herself up for air as he applied more effort to keep her underneath the water. Just long enough. The struggle continued, but Poppy could feel herself begin to lose strength. And then her will began to fade. *Fifty three years. That was going to be it? That was all she was allocated in this life? She was far from ready to die. And there certainly had to be a better way to go than to be murdered. Murdered in the waters that took the life of her little brother. My God, she surely did not return to the island, to this very cottage, to lose her life in this horrific manner.*

Her body went limp. She sunk, what felt like much lower, in the ocean water. Her eyes were closed, but she willed herself to open them again. It was difficult to see anything underneath the water. The salt water burned her eyes. That was a good thing though. She wanted to feel something, anything. She needed to believe that she still had some fight left in her. Poppy knew that was true. She prayed to God, she called out to Bobby in her mind in the midst of that prayer. A part of her was ready to see him again, but not like this. Not now. Not yet.

She tried to swim. *Upward, Poppy. Swim up to the dock. Swim the length of it, and then surface. You can hold onto it until he's gone. You can breathe again, you can surface, if you swim now. Do it!* She heard the voice inside of her head. It was Bobby. She was certain of it. Either he was helping her, or she had lost her mind. She would listen though. And if she failed, as least she would die trying.

Poppy swam upward. She forced her legs and her arms to work hard. It felt like useless effort to her. She must have really sunk low to the bottom. The fears she held as a child of her brother's drowning resurfaced. *Was the ocean bottomless? Why couldn't they ever find Bobby?* Poppy forced herself to focus. *Focus on swimming. Surface. Get some damn air in your lungs!*

She was getting somewhere. Her limbs burned. The muscles in her arms and legs felt strained and sore. She pushed harder. She could have cried, but it would have taken up too much energy. Energy she didn't have to spare. The darkness under the water began to fade, there was light again. It was the sunlight on the water. She was close. Close to the surface. Poppy could see the dock now, above her. She swam the length of it. And finally, she reached the end and grabbed ahold of it. Her head was above the water. She could breathe, but it was almost as if she had forgotten how. She choked, she coughed, she gagged, all the while clinging to the wood on the dock. She felt splinters pricking her fingers, but she only grasped tighter. And that's when she thought her efforts to save herself had all been for nothing. Two strong hands suddenly grabbed her from above, on the dock. She panicked and she fought —her arms flailing, her hoarse screams— until she heard another voice trying to reach her.

"Poppy, it's okay. You're okay. It's Kirk. Grab ahold of my hands. I'm going to pull you up."

She was safe. She focused on the police uniform he was wearing. The chief. Her childhood crush. Oak Bluffs Chief of Police. Kirk had her back, just as he told her he would. He had been right to distrust Dudley Connors.

Chapter twenty

It took everything Poppy had left in her being to lift up her arms. She saw Kirk's face, she felt the strength of his upper body as he grabbed ahold of her and pulled. He lifted her up, out of the water. She was lying flat on her back on the fishing dock. She was drenched and freezing. She felt her body trembling uncontrollably. And the last thing she remembered seeing was Dudley face down on the dock, just a short distance from her. She saw his arms pinned behind his back, and there were handcuffs locked at his wrists. And then Poppy's world went dark.

✝✝✝

When Poppy opened her eyes, her body ached. The room was bright, her vision was blurred. She found it difficult to inhale a complete breath. She was in bed, a hospital bed. A room she must have been lying in alone, for who knows how long. Poppy focused her eyes on the chair next to the bed on which she laid, blanketed up to her chin. It was an armchair. Tealy was sitting on it, with her legs pulled up to her chest. And next to her, straddled on the arm of the chair, was CeCe. Her girls came. *How did they know? Was she near death, was that why someone called them?* As Poppy stirred, she caught their attention.

"Mom's awake!" CeCe jumped to her feet, and Tealy followed her to Poppy's bedside.

"Gir...l...s," Poppy tried to speak, but there was something covering her mouth and nose. She reached her hand up to it. *A tube, an oxygen mask.*

"Oh my God, mom! You scared us so bad," Tealy was the first to take her mother's hand. Poppy tried to squeeze it back.

Poppy never responded. What happened to her on the dock was beginning to come back, and then all at once she remembered. A few machines started sound off around her, and above her head.

"Stay calm," CeCe told her. "I'll get the doctor in here."

✂ ✂ ✂

When a middle-aged man, with wavy graying hair, in a long white lab coat, walked into the room, he was followed by CeCe. Poppy looked twice. Reed was behind the both of them.

She pulled at her oxygen mask. "Seriously? What are you doing here?" Her words came out slower than normal, but she managed to spit them out to express her disapproval of her ex-husband's presence. The doctor glanced back at Reed, and then at Poppy's daughters. They just shook their heads, as if to dismiss Poppy's question. The doctor seemed to accept that.

"Good to see you awake, you took a long forty-eight hour nap," the doctor spoke as he checked the pupils of her eyes.

Two days? She had been asleep, out cold, for two days?

The doctor, who smelled strongly of cologne and mint gum, continued to speak to Poppy. You took in some water in those lungs of yours, but mild hypothermia was what put you in this bed and comatose for awhile. That's common after a near-drowning episode." *Drowning. She damn near drowned. Just like Bobby. Dudley tried to kill her in that water. Oh my God...where was he now?*

When the doctor completely removed the oxygen mask from Poppy's face, she looked at him and then around the room at both of her daughters, and finally at Reed standing with his back up against a far wall. He knew Poppy would not welcome him there. *But he had to come.*

"Do you remember what happened?" the doctor asked her.

"I do," Poppy nodded. She felt hot tears fill up in her eyes. "He tried to kill me, drown me..." She wanted to know if he was in jail. *He. Dudley Connors. A man she befriended. Trusted. Slept with.* She did not want her family to know that about her. But it was obviously too late for that. Even still, Poppy felt ashamed. *Had she really been that vulnerable? Just when was beginning to feel stronger than she had in a very long time, the unimaginable happened.*

"Oh mom," she heard CeCe say, as the doctor began to speak again.

"The police chief is going to want to talk to you. We were asked to notify him when you were awake. If you do not feel up to speaking with him, just say the word, and I will delay that statement." The doctor was very kind, but Poppy wanted to talk to Kirk. She needed more information. *What happened out there on the beach, on the dock? How had Kirk managed to save her?* She recalled seeing Dudley restrained and handcuffed.

"It's fine, I'm okay. I need answers, too," Poppy told the doctor.

"And rest. You need rest. I will be back again later," he responded, and then left the hospital room.

"We also need answers, mom," Tealy spoke up. Poppy noticed Reed's silence. He knew better than to push it. His presence in that room was something Poppy was on the verge of not allowing. He knew it. He could see it on her face when she gave him fleeting eye contact. *Glares.* The only thing keeping him here thus far was the fact that she was weak and still comprehending all that had happened, and she was a little bit touched that he had traveled all the way there for her. *Or maybe he was there for moral support for the girls.*

She tried to move, in an attempt to possibly sit up in that bed, but she winced from pain. "My chest hurts," she told them.

"You had rescue breathing on the dock after the chief pulled you out of the water. The doctor said you may be a little bruised from the chest compressions," CeCe informed her.

"My goodness, that must have been quite a scene," Poppy stated, imagining the paramedics, the stretcher, and possibly even the ambulance in the sand. She never heard or saw anything. She had closed her eyes and that was it. A part of her wished she would have been conscious to see Dudley brought down to his knees. *Bastard. She had tried with everything she had to fight him. But it wasn't enough.*

"What were you doing with him?" Reed spoke, and it sounded like an accusation. As if Poppy was purposely hanging out with someone dangerous. The fact was, she truly believed Dudley was harmless.

Poppy shot him a look.

"Maybe I should rephrase that," Reed began again. "Was he watching you outside of your cottage? The officer, the chief who was here at the hospital twice since they brought you in, said he's the caretaker."

"I knew him," Poppy answered vaguely.

"None of that matters right now," Tealy shot a glance of disapproval at her father. "You need to concentrate on getting well, mom, that's all."

"Don't be so naïve," CeCe barked at her little sister. "Of course it matters. Mom is not safe here. That son of a bitch deserves to be locked up for the duration."

"I'd like to see to that," a voice spoke from the open doorway. They all saw a man in uniform. His short, once golden blond hair, was mostly all gray. His chest was broad, and the bullet proof vest underneath his uniform made him look incredibly buff. "Poppy...it's really good to see that you're awake."

"Thank you, Kirk," she spoke, and she could feel her family's eyes all on her. She realized how personable she and the chief had sounded with each other. For a moment Poppy could have smirked, having Reed in the room. Between dangerous Dudley and the heroic, handsome police chief, it looked as if Poppy was making some male friends on the island. That wasn't funny though — Dudley could have killed her.

"I have questions, you have answers that I need on record. Your doctor said you're ready and able," Kirk began, as she moved closer to her bedside. Her family was suddenly pushed to the background. Kirk sensed her uneasiness and spoke.

"Your family can stay, it's your call," he told her, and waited.

They were going to find out the truth, the entire story, eventually. She believed it may be easier not to have to retell the story again later to all of them. *Well, to her girls. She really didn't owe Reed an explanation, or anything.*

"It's fine," she agreed.

159

Kirk pulled the armchair closer to the bed and then plopped down on it. Poppy wanted to smile. He hadn't changed much. At fourteen years old, she remembered him as being at ease, and comfortable in his own skin. He could make himself feel at home anywhere. She laughed at the thought of him lying on the pastel plaid sofa in the cottage's living room after a swim. Julie Blare had walked in, surprised by his presence, and taken aback by the forward teenager in their summer home.

She watched him flip an old fashioned notepad and grab a pen from his shirt pocket. "When we spoke at Lookout Tavern, you told me Dudley was a friend. I already knew he was the caretaker of the beach cottages. You were having dinner with him. I warned you to be careful. I saw what happened after we parted ways and you went back to your table," Kirk stated.

"He had left. The waitress told me he was watching the two of us, talking, and cancelled our dinner order, paid for the drinks, and left the restaurant." If Poppy had only known how unstable and dangerous he was.

"I followed you back to the cottage, to make sure you got home safe," Kirk told her, and she gave him a sincere smile.

"I was safe. I went home fearing he might show up, but he didn't. He did call me though, and he apologized for running out on me at dinner," Poppy said, on the record.

"And that was that? He didn't push you for anything else?" Kirk asked.

"He wanted to come by for a drink, but I told him no. I said I had a headache from not eating and I was going to grab a bite and go to bed." Kirk smiled to himself, as he had made reference at the restaurant to Poppy about women and how they needed to make necessary excuses sometimes.

"Had you gone out with him before?" Poppy knew Kirk was looking for specifics.

"Gone out, no," Poppy began. "We had a few talks on beach, and at the cottage shortly after I arrived on island. One night we shared two bottles of wine in my kitchen."

"So, you and he had gotten drunk?" Kirk was straightforward. He sounded more like a police chief than her old friend from the summer of 1976.

"He didn't seem the slightest bit, no," Poppy answered truthfully. "I was relaxed, borderline tipsy." Poppy thought she saw a little smile on the chief's face.

"Did anything happen between the two of you that night?" It was a fair question, but Poppy more than hesitated to answer. She looked at her daughters' faces. They were listening raptly. She tried not to look at Reed, but she did anyway. Crushed was an accurate description of his body language and the look on his face. *His Poppy was dating other men. Well, she was no longer his.*

Poppy inhaled a slow, deep breath. "Yes," she answered. "It's going to come as a shock to my family, my children and my ex-husband in this room..." Poppy was sure to clarify that she and Reed were divorced. *Why did she want Kirk to know that? For no other reason than for him to believe she was a woman of character. She was not an adulteress. She had a one night stand because she was lonely and incredibly turned on by someone other than her husband of twenty-eight years who betrayed her for most of*

161

their married life. "I slept with Dudley that night."

Poppy watched her girls exchange looks. And this time she never looked over at Reed.

Tealy immediately judged her mother, silently in her thoughts. *Oh my God. This woman is not my mother. My mother has self respect and honorable values.*

CeCe had her own opinion regarding this information about her mother. *You go girl! It's about time you lived a little.* The fact that the man her mother chose to do the deed with was obsessive and dangerous did scare CeCe immensely, but the idea of her mother momentarily letting go of her grief, and her holier than thou persona, was refreshing to her. Of course CeCe was wild at heart. She would root for anyone to let loose, even though there's always irreversible consequences. And sometimes pain.

Reed walked out of the room. Poppy tried to act as if his leaving did not bother her, but it had. She was certain he was breaking inside. She knew him well. He could do whatever he damn well pleased but, to him, Poppy would remain all-good, sweet and pure. *Damn you, she thought. Don't make me feel guilty after all you put me through.* The fact was, it wasn't Reed or her daughters who made Poppy feel at fault and accountable for her shocking actions. It was herself.

"I know this is personal," Kirk spoke gently, "but did it only happen once? Did you sleep with him again after that night?"

"Just once," Poppy was quick to answer. "I wasn't sure if I wanted it to happen again. And then I started to notice him watching me — from the dock on the beach, at Lookout Tavern when I was having lunch with my girls. I don't know if he followed me to the grocery store the night I accepted his dinner invitation and saw you, but he was there when I was. He just started to act too aggressive. There were no boundaries or respect with him after we slept together. I felt uneasy about him, I guess you could say."

"What took place on the dock the morning he tried to drown you?" Those words strung together sounded awful to Poppy. The memory of it actually happening brought tears to her eyes." Kirk reached up and squeezed her knee through the white thermal blanket on the hospital bed. "Take your time," he spoke softly. It wasn't a gesture from a police chief questioning her, it was comfort from an old friend.

"I took a long walk on the beach, and when I returned to the cottage, I saw him sitting on the dock, watching me, waiting for me. I confronted him. I was forthright, and maybe even heartless. I felt like I had to be, because I wasn't getting through to him. He told me he was falling in love with me, and he got angry when I told him I didn't reciprocate those feelings, and I wanted space. I wanted him to leave me alone."

Poppy watched the chief of police scribbling notes onto the pad of paper. He looked up at her as she continued on.

"He charged me. He grabbed me with both of his hands. He was choking the air out of me." Poppy reached up to touch her throat. She didn't know it, but there were marks there, now red and purple and bruise-like. Tealy covered her mouth with her own hand and looked down at the floor. CeCe looked stronger, and able to handle hearing what happened to her mother, but it broke her heart to know she suffered at the hands of a maniac — and no one had been there to save her. Not until the Oak Bluffs police chief arrived.

"You got away from his choke hold — you fought him off?" Kirk was looking for specifics.

"Yes, I forced my knee into his groin. But when I tried to get away, I was lightheaded from being deprived of air and I fell. The dock, the boards were broken through by Dudley's foot in a fit of rage. I fell through that hole."

"I saw," Kirk told her.

"Excuse me?" Poppy was confused, but then she realized Kirk must have meant he saw the broken boards on the dock after he arrived and rescued her. But that's not what he was about to explain.

"I was on duty that morning and feeling on edge about Dudley Connors. Something just didn't feel right about leaving you alone in that cottage. He had an obsession with you, so I was watching him. He sat on that dock for hours. He was there when you left for your walk on the beach, but you never looked that way, never saw him. I waited for you to return, because I knew he was waiting. I saw the confrontation between the two of you. I made my way closer when I saw him choking you. I saw you fall. Seconds passed. I hoped to God he was going to pull you up, through that hole. When he didn't, when I witnessed him trying to drown you, I charged up that beach, and onto the dock. You had already gone under, way under. Thank God you could swim, and were able to surface on your own."

"You restrained Dudley and saved me," Poppy finished his story.

"No, you saved yourself. I just pulled you up, out of the water and onto that dock." Kirk was being modest. He was the one who saved her. She was out of strength. She remembered wanting to give up, knowing she was so close to doing just that. She also knew she lost consciousness. And Kirk had been there to take care of her. If he had not had his man of the law instincts and was not there watching Dudley, Poppy would not have been saved at all. She would have died in that water.

"Thank you," Poppy spoke softly, and Kirk nodded his head. There was no thanks necessary.

Chapter twenty-one

Kirk, as the official police chief, left her hospital room. He said he would be in touch before she was released from the hospital. He squeezed Poppy's hand, and called her a *strong and incredibly brave woman.*

Before he left, Poppy asked him what would come of Dudley. *Did he already have his freedom?* Kirk informed both Poppy and her daughters that Dudley Connors was behind bars and would stay there until his attempted murder trial.

Both CeCe and Tealy were sitting on the hospital bed, one daughter on each side of their mother. "I'm so sorry this happened to you," Poppy heard CeCe say. "We're just so relieved that you are okay," Tealy added.

"Should I go and see where dad went?" CeCe offered, and Poppy's eyes widened.

"You do what you want to do when it comes to your father, both of you," Poppy also looked at Tealy. "As my ex-husband, he shouldn't even be here."

"He still cares, mom," CeCe defended her father.

"And I still care as well," she spoke honestly, "but that's where it ends. There's nothing he can do for me here. Maybe he just wanted to rush to my bedside for the sake of you girls, or maybe he wanted the chance to say goodbye, had I been dying."

"Mom, stop," Tealy spoke up. "I don't understand any of you, really. Dad had another family practically all of mine and C's lives, CeCe was screwing around with her best friend's man, and now you are taking your clothes off for complete strangers! I feel like I'm the only normal one in the bunch. My whole family is fucked up!" Poppy allowed her youngest daughter to speak. She had every right to say what she did. But then Poppy also had something to say to her.

"Be careful. Fairytales do not last forever," Poppy warned Tealy. "Look what I thought I had."

"What are you trying to tell me?" Tealy appeared worried.

"Nothing other than the fact that happiness can be short-lived, and nobody is perfect." Poppy looked at CeCe as she finished speaking. *What she said could not have been truer.*

"She's also trying to tell you to get off your high horse," CeCe jabbed at Tealy, and Tealy attempted to push her off of the bed as she said, "Go to hell!"

"Girls!" Poppy scolded them as if they were children again. "You two should go grab some lunch. I know how cranky you get when you're hungry. Maybe see if your father wants to eat as well."

"Still looking out for him, aren't you?" CeCe stated as a matter of fact.

"Go," Poppy ordered. "I need to rest." She closed her eyes as her girls promised they would be back soon.

⺅⺅⺅

Poppy spent the following twenty-four hours in the hospital before she was finally released. She still felt sore, but stronger, and she was ready to return to her temporary life at the cottage. Both CeCe and Tealy had been back and forth from the hospital to the cottage, as Poppy had insisted they stay there. They had spent the first two days on island at Poppy's bedside, fearful that she would never wake up, or worse.

Reed had not been back to the hospital, and Poppy didn't ask her girls about him. It was easier that way, to just not talk about him. CeCe was driving her SUV with Poppy in the passenger seat and Tealy in the middle captain's chair. She watched CeCe look into the rearview mirror at Tealy, but she never spoke. After she did this a second time, Poppy called out both of them.

"Okay, what is it? The two of you have something to tell me. I know the look, the silent glances. Out with it!" It felt good to be their mother again, when they were all together like this. Poppy knew, however, that they would have to return to their own lives very soon. They had already spent days on the island, by her side.

"I'm not telling her," Tealy spoke up, as stubborn and righteous as always.

CeCe rolled her eyes. "Dad's still here," she blurted outright.

"Here? As in on island?" Poppy questioned her oldest daughter directly.

"Nope, here, as in at the cottage." CeCe held her breath as she turned her vehicle, which dipped down into a low parking lot near the beachfront cottages.

"Oh no, no way! I refuse to let him stay. I can't believe he's been staying there all this time without my consent. Jesus! I am so damn mad right now!" Poppy knew she needed to relax, but this news rattled her.

"Just breathe," Tealy offered from the middle seat. "I was upset too, at first, but he means well. He's worried about you. He said he would leave as soon as you are settled. We actually all have to leave as soon as you are settled and on the road to recovery." Poppy knew that Tealy's young family was waiting for her. CeCe's job awaited her. And Reed had his practice—

someone, somewhere needed oral surgery.

Poppy kept silent as they parked, walked through the sand, and then onto the boardwalk. As if he knew he wouldn't be welcomed inside in Poppy's presence, Reed was seated on the boardwalk in a lounge chair. He was wearing athletic black pants and a red hoodie, with no shoes or socks. The sun was bright, but the air was chilly. Poppy again was barefoot in flip flips and also wearing a comfortable winter white sweatsuit that the girls brought to the hospital for her to wear home.

"Go inside girls," was all Poppy said.

"Seriously? We're not five," Tealy said under her breath, and Poppy heard CeCe giggle. They did as she asked, and closed the cottage door behind them. Poppy didn't hesitate to sit down in the empty lounge chair, adjacent to Reed's. She was worn out. She wouldn't admit it, but she felt like she had been to hell and back the past few days.

"You look good, better than when we first got here," Reed spoke to her. "You really scared me, Poppy. I thought you were going to leave us."

"I've already left you," she added in a deliberate snarky tone.

"Yes, you have," he nodded. She watched him, sitting there. He had some reading material on his lap, and his reading glasses were still low on his nose. He was beginning to show the characteristics of an old man. *Gone was the young, vibrant man, who could sometimes be cocky and arrogant. A surgeon. A rich man. A confident man. A man who could have any woman he wanted, two in his life at a time in fact.* There was no other way to describe

Reed now, other than aged and broken.

"I thought you had left the island," Poppy stated. "I'm fine now. You can go home."

"Home?" he asked her.

"It's where your children are," she spoke with certainty. He had three children, a son too. That still pained her more than ever.

"It is," he agreed. "Can I ask you something, Poppy?"

"I guess," she answered.

"Do you ever look back and think about the time we first met...when we promised each other the world?" Reed's mood was melancholy as he spoke.

More than you know. "What would be the point of that now?" she asked him, bluntly.

"The point is, you have no regrets. You didn't break any of those promises that we made to each other. You excelled to perfection. I was the one who failed."

"If I was so damn perfect in your eyes, then why? Why Reed?" She had not asked him that before. Not in the days, weeks, or months, leading up to their divorce. Not once had she wanted to talk this out with him. It just didn't seem worth it. Pointless. But now, it seemed fitting. They had nothing to lose. They had already lost each other, and their life together.

"Power. The attention, the affection powered my ego. I got in way over my head, and then I was stuck. I had a son on the way. I could not turn my back on him. I knew if you knew, I would lose the family I already had. Our family. I negotiated my personal life like a business man. I supported her and my son. I helped raise him."

"All the while you were also playing family with me and our girls. You were sleeping in our bed while you were also touching her and making love to her. Was that what it was with her, Reed? Was it love or was it sex?" She really didn't want him to answer that. She had been there when he leaned over her corpse in that casket. *It was clearly some form of love.*

"Sex, at first," he admitted, "but I did care." That was the safest way he knew how to explain this to Poppy. She was his gentle, caring wife. The other woman was anything but gentle and she really had not cared about anyone other than herself and her son. The forbidden sex between them was explosive, but that had faded over time. She gave him blowjobs. She bent over the chair for him to take her in ways he never experienced with his wife at home. It had to be different with his mistress, because he never wanted to think of Poppy while he was with her.

"I never really cared about the physical part of our relationship," she admitted, knowing all too well she hadn't spoken anything like that to him before.

"I know," he stated.

"So you needed more? You went looking for blowjobs and a woman to go down on you?" Poppy felt sickened. *How could this have been partly her fault? And why was she allowing herself to remotely acknowledge that?*

"My God… Poppy… If I could take it all back…" Reed started to say.

"Stop it. If I could bring my brother back, I would. We can't. It's life. It sucks, but we have to deal with tragedies, choices, and those godawful consequences." Poppy was the smartest, strongest woman Reed had ever known. *Had he ever told her that?*

"You're right," he told her. "So how do I live the rest of my life like this? I am lost. You were my beacon."

"I believe that was the other way around. That's why I'm here on this island, at this cottage. Along with the fact that I needed to return to the place where my life changed as a twelve-year-old girl, I also needed to find my way alone. Without you as my flare. I guess, considering what happened, I am failing at taking care of myself."

"Not true," Reed told her, despite the fact that he had been beating himself up about being the reason she was alone and vulnerable. "You can hold your own, Poppy Brennan. You always could. And in the process you've held me up as well as our daughters." She smiled at the compliment. *There could be some truth to her ex-husband's compliment.*

"Did you sleep with him to get back at me?" There it was. The question that Poppy had wanted to steer clear of with Reed. It was none of his business, and her answer in any form would be hurtful. They needed to be finished with causing each other pain.

"Reed, please. That's personal."

"We were married. You cannot get more personal than that," he told her.

"We're divorced. Most things become private again when that happens." Poppy smiled a little. "But, I know what you are asking of me. I've actually asked the same thing of myself. I'm going to tell you the truth. I'm not saying this to hurt you. I'm saying it because you asked and we are on a roll here with spilling our innermost thoughts." This time, Reed smiled. "You were the farthest person from my mind when I let another man touch me. I had sex on the floor of my ancestor's cottage. I had the most explosive orgasm in my life — with a stranger. I did it because I wanted to live in the moment. I wanted to feel. This numbness that I've been carrying around with me is slowly killing me. I just lived in the moment, Reed," she restated. "That's all. There's a first time for everything. Even for me."

"That's torture for me to imagine," Reed admitted. "My Poppy. My wife. But, I understand what you just told me. I am the guiltiest person alive when it comes to living in the moment. I do, in a very strange way, feel comforted knowing you lost your head for awhile."

"I'm human, too," she told her ex-husband.

"I've never been convinced of that," he teased. "Super human, maybe."

"Go back to Boston, Reed. Find happiness." Those may have been the most sincere words Poppy had ever said to him.

"I'll worry about you," he stated, like a man who still wanted to protect her.

"I'm a big girl," she reminded him, like a woman trying to be stronger than she felt.

"I'll miss you for the rest of my life," Reed told her, as he made the effort to reach out his hand from his chair to hers.

She took it. She held his hand with hers. The comfort of that gesture had not changed. That feeling had not been lost or stolen from them. His was the hand she once believed she would hold with hers until the end of time. The thought of that now brought tears to her eyes.

"And I'll love you for the rest of mine," she said to him.

Chapter twenty-two

Their once family of four stayed one night at the cottage together before they separated again as the broken family that they now were. Broken seemed like such a harsh description, and maybe it wasn't so harsh between them anymore. The exchange that Poppy and Reed shared on the boardwalk was open, raw, honest, and genuine. Reed was remorseful. And Poppy was beginning to open her heart to forgiveness. She would never forget, nor would she ever completely understand. She just wanted to choose peace, and she believed she had. She could have chosen to spend years feeling angry and bitter, but why?

After Reed and Tealy left the island together, Poppy was going to spend one additional day with CeCe. "You'd think I would learn to stop volunteering to drive here, because I always have to give up my vehicle when I end up staying another day," CeCe teased her mother when they returned to the cottage from the ferry.

"You just want an excuse to see the rug rats," Poppy chided, using CeCe's not-so-endearing term for them.

"Maybe I do," CeCe winked, and Poppy laughed out loud.

"Let's get some wine and sit outside," Poppy suggested.

"I'll pour you a glass. I need a clear head for the conversation we are going to have," CeCe stated.

Poppy was beyond concerned for her oldest daughter. "I'm here for you, no matter what. Tell me how much you miss him, and I'll understand. Tell me you're sorry for hurting Jen and for being a part of the reason that pushed her over the edge — and I'll side with you and comfort you, even though I understand her pain more." Poppy watched CeCe pour a generous stemless glass of wine, and she gratefully took if from her as they stepped outside. But when they realized it was raining, sleeting in spots, they turned around to go back inside to lounge on the white suede sofa.

"I'll need you to just listen, okay?" CeCe forewarned her mother.

"There's really nothing left that could shock me or hurt me, is there?" Poppy asked, and when CeCe didn't answer her, she sighed, and waited. She would listen now.

"Dad and I are close because we understand each other. There was a time though, when I hated him." Poppy looked as if she didn't believe her daughter. "I was sixteen, and remember that amazing BMW convertible that dad bought me?" How could Poppy ever forget? She argued that it was too extravagant for a girl, brand new to the driving scene. As a teenager, Poppy had been forced to work to afford her first car — despite the fact that her father was a wealthy judge. Reed protested and eventually won. "I was driving around, almost past curfew one night, when I spotted Dad at the office. He was driving away actually, so I followed him. I didn't realize it at the time, but he wasn't alone in his vehicle." Poppy felt the color drain from her face. "I saw him with her...I confronted him. I told him I was going to tell you. It's not that he forced me to keep quiet. He just painted a very sad picture of how our lives would be if we weren't a family anymore." Poppy was crying now. "Fifteen years later, the truth came out. And, guess what? Dad was right. Our family was immediately no more." CeCe reached for Poppy's hand on her lap. "I don't know if I should say I'm sorry, because I honestly do not even know if I am. I mean, I bought us more than a decade longer together as a family."

Poppy was silent for longer than CeCe was comfortable with.

"This secret, this truth you've been keeping to yourself for far too long, puts a few things into perspective for me," Poppy was still crying as she spoke. "My poor girl. You were saddled with something entirely too big for you. Too all-consuming for your mind and your heart. You should have come to me. Instead, this burden formed you. Look at your choices. Your life with Stu Brentwood never could have continued as it was, but you believed so. I blame your father for this, not you."

CeCe was the one crying now. "Wonderful. Just when the two of you are mending a little, I go and give you a reason to hate him again." CeCe sniffed and then cried harder. Poppy reached for her and pulled her close.

"I'm not angry with you, and my disappointment for your father really cannot get much worse. It's you I'm worried about. What's your game plan?" Poppy knew her daughter well. She lived day to day in preparation for what lied ahead. CeCe, up until most recently, truly believed she was going to live out a happy life in secret with Stu. And she had been content with that notion. She had already been living much of that sort of life with him for three years. It saddened Poppy beyond words to think that Reed had taught their daughter that it was okay to deceive.

CeCe laughed through her tears. "If I've learned anything from this mess, it's that you can't plan for a damn thing to go as you've prepared for. I no longer have Stu to love, and yes I did love him. I still have my career. I have you and dad, and that shithead of a sister of mine." Poppy laughed. "And I'll have my future with my baby. I'm pregnant, mom."

Chapter twenty-three

The shock had truly yet to wear off a day later when Poppy drove CeCe to catch the ferry. She would again take a cab to Tealy's house to pick up her vehicle. No one else besides Poppy knew about the pregnancy yet, and CeCe wanted to keep the news quiet for a little while. Poppy felt privileged to know, and she promised her first born that everything was going to be okay. There was a reason she was bringing a child into this world.

CeCe swore time and again that she never wanted to have children, but her view on that seemed to have abruptly changed once she discovered she would have a part of Stu left in this world, a son or daughter that would tie her to him lifelong. Poppy worried that it was unhealthy for her to worship a child for the sake of its DNA. She pushed those thoughts out of her mind, and swore she would be right by CeCe's side as her life was about to be altered forever in just a matter of months.

Another visit that had drawn them closer as mother and daughter had come to an end, and Poppy once again returned to the cottage alone. She wondered how long that would last this time and laughed to herself about how her intentions of being by herself hadn't entirely panned out.

Her cell phone was already ringing a few minutes after she walked in the door. She wasn't utilizing the deadbolt anymore, as she felt safe again knowing the only person on earth who was ever a threat to her was in a jail cell. That fact still seemed surreal to her, too. But it was real. She had the marks on her neck to remind her. The consuming fear that Poppy had running through her entire body in that moment, knowing Dudley had turned on her and wanted her to die in that water, was something she would never forget, but sure wished she could.

She didn't recognize the caller ID number on her home screen. "Hello?"

"Poppy, it's Kirk. I'm calling on official police business. Is this a good time for you?"

"Of course," she told him, "but that line scares me a little. Please tell me there's not a reason for me to lock my door again.

Is Dudley still in custody?"

"For now, yes," Kirk replied. "He flunked his psychiatric evaluation."

"And that's not a good thing?" Poppy was confused.

"Not in the case when we want to lock him up indefinitely," Kirk attempted to explain. "This could keep Dudley out of prison. And, if you ask me, I think he's one of the smart ones. He knows exactly what he's doing to avoid prison — despite the fact that I saw him try to kill you."

"So what can I do?"she asked Kirk. "Besides pack up and leave this island." The very last thing Poppy wanted to do was run. She didn't want to allow Dudley to make that decision for her. To chase her way.

"You're not serious, are you?" Kirk asked her, and she wondered if he was asking as an old friend or as the chief of police.

"I don't want to be," she admitted.

"You'll have to stay, or at least come back, if this case goes to trial. And that's why I'm calling actually, to ask you to be prepared to testify. To lock this case we are going to need your face, your words, on that stand in the court of law."

"I already told you everything, on the record," she said, as if he needed to be reminded.

"I'll be with you every step of the way," he offered.

"I don't like this. I didn't want to have to see him again." Poppy was terrified of that happening and had talked herself out of it ever occurring when Kirk told her that Dudley was in jail.

"I hear you, and once I have a talk with the psychiatrist on Dudley's case, I'll know more. Just stay put on island, okay?"

Why did Poppy suddenly feel as if she was the prisoner? "Yes, sir," she teased, and heard him laugh on the opposite end of the phone.

"Good girl. Talk soon."

✂ ✂ ✂

It was an expression. *Talk soon.* What Poppy had not expected was for Kirk to call her back as *soon* as two hours later. This time, she recognized his number, and didn't answer blindly.

He got right to the point of his second call. "Poppy, I'm in your neighborhood, would it be okay if I stopped by? It's business," he added. Kirk Lane was a man of the law, but he had waited too long for Dudley Connors to screw up again, and this time he wasn't going to allow him to slip through his fingers. Even if it meant bending the rules. It was time that he told Poppy what his personal connection was to that man. Because, in Kirk's mind, taking away his freedom was past due.

"Yes," she said, after a few seconds of hesitation. It was too cold outside to meet him on the boardwalk, or at the beach. She would have to welcome him into the cottage. Poppy didn't know why, but she felt apprehensive about that. She blamed Dudley for making her feel anxious.

He knocked, and Poppy was waiting to open the door. He stood there on the front porch in full police uniform, bullet proof vest and all. "Hi, come in." Poppy spoke first.

When Kirk stepped inside, he smiled. "Seriously? This place hasn't changed all that much. It's like going back in time."

Poppy laughed. "I felt the very same way when I walked in here after four decades. There's just something about a place that retains its special feel, if you know what I mean."

"I do now," Kirk told her.

"Can I get you a drink, water or something?" She assumed he was on duty.

"No, but thanks," he replied. "Let's sit though," he added, making the first move to walk toward the white suede sofa and sit down. Poppy laughed to herself. He was still very much the Kirk she remembered. She sat next to him, and he spoke again.

"I found out, in detail, how Dudley's psychiatric eval went. I had a one-on-one visit with the professional who has, in my opinion, a spot on judgment of our criminal." It still alarmed Poppy to know that Dudley was dangerous. "He's playing us. He knows how to beat the system. Every single answer makes him out on paper to be bat shit crazy. He went as far as to speak as if his wife just died. He stated the current year, but he acts as if he just lost her."

Poppy shook her head. "Is it even true that she died of MS? Or was that a lie or fabrication of some sort, too?"

"That's true, but again it was three years ago," Kirk reminded her. "Poppy, I'm here on official police business to tell you that Dudley will not go to prison when a judge gets ahold of that psychiatric report. He'll see six months to a year max in a mental institution. I'm also here as Kirk, your buddy from the beach way back when." Poppy smiled and creased her brow at the same time. *What was he getting at?* "I need your help to nail him."

"You're not making complete sense. I feel like there's more to Dudley, more to what you know about him than you're sharing with me," Poppy spoke, honestly. This was her sitting on a sofa with an old friend, not the Oak Bluffs police chief. She wasn't even sure what he wanted her to do, or how she could possibly help. What she was certain of was she wanted the truth from him. *What had honestly made her old friend stop her in a public place to warn her about the man she was having dinner with?*

"You're perceptive," he complimented her, and Poppy thought — *Not so much, if you knew my life story.*

"Sit back. This could take awhile," he said. "My wife and I were having some issues a couple of years back," he paused to clear his throat. So now Poppy knew Kirk was married. *Of course he was.* "Long story short, she claimed I was more committed to being the chief than I was to her. I fell short. I see my faults now. But then, I was angry and hurt. She cheated on me with Dudley Connors. She was vulnerable, and he played on that. It's what he does, Poppy." Her eyes widened. *She was his victim all along? Their attraction, their in-the-moment sex on the floor of the cottage had been a part of his plan with her?* "He was obsessed with my wife. She wanted to break things off. She and I were going to mend our marriage, or at least make an attempt to save what we both wanted to fight for. Dudley wouldn't leave her alone. He followed her everywhere. He was pushy to the point where I issued a restraining order against him. He was not supposed to come within fifty feet of my wife. And he tested that like you wouldn't believe. And then one morning, two years ago, my wife was in a single car accident on her way to work. She was killed." Poppy covered her mouth with her hand. The shock of this left her speechless.

"A witness, who did not want to go on the record, saw Dudley's car in the area parked along that very same roadside during the exact time frame that my wife had the accident. I searched every half inch of that road, but I couldn't prove he was there. Not a damn tire track, nothing. My wife was one of the most careful, cautious drivers. She didn't just drive off of the road. She was run off, with the intent to kill."

"Oh my God, I don't have the words, Kirk."

"I know," he shook his head. "You can help me get him now. I will keep you safe, but I want to avenge my wife's death. I've given up on doing this by the book. I thought we had him, but we need more."

"What can I possibly do?" Poppy asked, feeling scared of what he would tell her. Terrified of what Kirk thought she was capable of pulling off. If Dudley was a smart criminal, he would see right through any ploy.

"I'm going to see to it that he's released from jail and placed in an institution immediately. And, if you're willing, you're going to pay him a visit at his new, but temporary home. You'll be wearing a wire," he added, and he noticed Poppy had looked down at her hands on her lap. They were clasped together tightly. He was certain they were clammy and cold. Her nerves had already gotten the best of her. And Kirk didn't blame her. This was risky. Dudley Connors was dangerous.

Chapter twenty-four

"Kirk!" Poppy spoke firmly. She stopped him from talking because she wanted to have a word. Yes, Kirk probably remembered her as a nice, impressionable girl from his teenage past. Perhaps his inkling was much of the same now, considering she had been weak and vulnerable enough to be another victim of Dudley Connors'. This was going to feel new and possibly even intimidating to her, but Poppy defended herself. Her safety. Her right to say no. "I never wanted to see that man again. You assured me he'd see the inside of a jail cell for a long time. And now you're telling me, asking me as your old buddy, to put myself at risk. I can't help but feel like you're using me, too. This, for you, is personal. But, what about me? What happens if something goes wrong?"

"You're right," Kirk said, admiring her for the guts she'd shown right now. She didn't want to help him and she had every right to tell him to go to hell, right along with his risky plan. "What's in it for you? I get that you are asking me just that. Well, I'll tell you what you're gaining. Your safety here on the island, and inside of this very cottage where a deadbolt is a measly barrier to a man like Dudley. Your freedom is every bit as much at stake as his, if you want my honest opinion. He did not stop until my wife was dead. She didn't want him anymore, and so he made sure she was eliminated. It's the only way a crazed man can survive without his obsession. When it's gone, he moves on to his next target — and now that's you, Poppy."

"So what really is in it for me —if I agree to wear a wire and go to see him— is my life. I'll be saving my own life. That is what you're telling me, isn't it, chief?"

"I'm not going into this with you as the chief. I'm Kirk. I'm the man who will protect you at all cost. Poppy, I swear, I will not let anything happen to you. Are you in?"

She didn't hesitate with her answer this time. "Yes, I'm in." After all, this was her life.

✗ ✗ ✗

Of all things for it to be called, the mental health facility on Martha's Vineyard was dubbed the Daybreak Clubhouse. As if it was somewhere fun, a place to party.

Three days into Dudley's stay, Kirk drove Poppy there. It was a planned visit. Dudley was aware that Poppy wanted to see him, and he had agreed to accept her as a visitor. That was a good sign, Kirk had told her. *He still had an interest in her.* Or maybe his curiosity peaked for why Poppy wanted to see him. Either way, Poppy was beyond nervous. *What she was setting herself up for?*

The listening device bug was size equivalent to a paper clip, and it was underneath her shirt and fastened to the material at the center of her bra. What Poppy was doing felt real to her now.

She was quiet on the drive to the Daybreak Clubhouse. Kirk had driven her in his black Chevy Silverado. He was off duty, but packing heat. He told Poppy he would be close by, right in the next room from where she was scheduled to meet Dudley.

"Listen in, that's all I'm going to do. You know what to do and how to lead Dudley into a conversation that will hope-fully expose him as sane, but criminal." They had rehearsed this plan, practically night and day, but even still Poppy was tense. "And don't let him see your fear," Kirk added. Poppy nodded.

Before they entered the facility, Kirk pulled Poppy aside for one additional thing. His nervousness was evident in how he wouldn't stop talking. "Go in there believing in yourself. I never would have asked this of you had I not recognized your capability. If something goes wrong, use the code word." The code was to make mention of her little brother, Bob. If she shortened Bobby's name, Kirk would get her out of there. For any reason at all. "And most important," he caught her before she opened the door, "if this flops, if he's closed off or just wiser than we give him credit for, it's okay for us to leave here with-out a confession. I'll get him eventually."

Poppy smiled at him. It was a nervous, but grateful smile. Poppy was touched at how he was trying to ease her mind in the kindest of ways. *Just do your best. We get what we get.* But Poppy didn't want to settle for almost, or not good enough. Not this time.

Her brother had not been strong *enough,* so he never made it out of the water.

Her mother. She didn't trust Poppy *enough* to share her grief and teach her how to heal when she neglected to include her in all of those returns to the cottage.

Reed. Poppy, alone, and the children she gave him, wasn't *enough* for her husband.

Dudley. He was too much, too soon. And when Poppy had *enough,* he tried to end her life. If he couldn't have her, he wanted her gone.

Finally, Poppy had *enough.*

The Daybreak Clubhouse depicted what Poppy had seen on television and in the movies. It was a halfway house — or the politically correct term, a mental institution —through and through. The colors were solid. No prints. No patterns. Powder blue painted walls. Bright white large-tiled flooring. Navy blue medical scrubs worn as the uniform for all staff. Gray sweat pants, white t-shirts, and white tennis shoes appeared to label the patients. Faces were friendly, solemn, blank, and some were frightening. Kirk had told Poppy not to look around, just walk, but she had searched her surroundings with wide inquisitive eyes anyway. They checked in at the main desk, and were escorted down a long, narrow hallway. Without uttering a word, a young, black male orderly pointed at one door for Kirk. He separated from Poppy with a quick squeeze of her hand and direct eye contact. Kirk never spoke a word. He just gave her reassurance that he was there. And then, he lightened the tension when he winked at her. Poppy took a deep breath as she watched Kirk enter the room next door, and close it. The orderly then opened another door for Poppy, and led the way inside of the room where she knew she would find Dudley.

The color of the walls and the floor didn't change from the hallway to the private room. The room was small, but there seemed to be a lot crammed in there. A bed, one armchair in the corner, and a small table with two chairs in the opposite corner. There was a standard sized vertical window on the far wall, and Dudley was standing in front of it — with his back to her right now. Poppy felt her heartbeat quicken. She wondered if Kirk could hear it pounding away so very near the listening device clipped to her bra, between her breasts.

"Mr. Connors, you have a visitor!" The orderly spoke in a tone with more than a hint of annoyance. He clearly didn't love his job. Before the young man exited the room, he turned to Poppy. "Two loud knocks on the door will get you out of here when you're ready." Poppy nodded, and attempted to smile. *Kirk would get her the hell out of there— if it came to that.*

Poppy felt imprisoned when the door was sealed and the two of them were left in there alone. Dudley had yet to turn around. She could hear her own pulse in her ears now. *Calm down, Poppy. Do not let him see your fear.*

Kirk was just on the other side of the wall. He knew the orderly had left, as he heard the door close. The silence heightened how nerve wracked he felt. *Someone say something. The damn device better not fail us!*

Poppy spoke first. "Dudley," she was surprised at how calm her voice sounded to herself. He turned around slowly. Without a baseball cap, he looked like a different man. The brown curls, speckled with graying hairs, took her back to the one time she did see him hatless. They were having sex on the floor of her cottage. Poppy blinked the thought away quickly, but then she wondered if that was wise. Maybe she should channel that moment, or the times with him when she trusted him. Liked him. She had to be convincing to him right now. "I can't believe this is happening to you."

Dudley looked perplexed. Kirk listened from the other side of the wall. Of course there were things she would adlib, but he already was a bit taken aback by how Poppy was starting this off.

"This place beats a jail cell," Dudley stated, as he remained standing in front of the window. Both of his feet were planted on the floor. His arms hung straight down at his sides. It was strange for Poppy to see him in thick soled white shoes. Flip flops had been the norm for him (and her) at the beach and on the island.

"I didn't think you belonged there either," she told him. Kirk was about to come unglued. This was not what they planned. *What the hell was she doing?* He stood with his back against the wall that separated the two rooms. He had no other choice but to trust Poppy — and what she was doing. She

193

already was off the map though, and he feared she couldn't handle this detour.

Poppy saw the interest in his eyes. She baited him. She knew it. But when he spoke, he appeared as if he was the one still very much in control. "Why are you here, Poppy?"

"I want the truth. I keep hearing what happened to me. That police chief will not lay off. He wants you put away for a very long time. I can't go along with a story I do not believe. This is the only place I knew to come. I want to know what happened to me. I know I can get answers here. When I first arrived on island, you were the one person who I could talk to. My constant. We connected. Now, please, help me remember what happened on that dock."

"Remember?" Dudley asked her. Again, she could see in his eyes how she had sent his mind reeling. And Kirk was on the other side of the wall with wide eyes and this time his heart rate was off the charts and pounding in his ears.

"I can't remember anything about that day other than my walk and finding you on the dock when I returned. We were talking, I have no idea what about. The next thing I recall in my cloudy mind is waking up in a hospital bed with my daughters at my bedside — and that police chief telling me that you tried to kill me." There it was. Poppy had forcefully thrown the ball with both hands, right into his.

"That son of a bitch is the reason I do not have my freedom!" Dudley spat. For a moment, he lost his calm and Poppy caught a glimpse of exactly the man who surfaced when he made the vicious attempts to take her life. First, with his hands around her throat. And second, when he forced and held her head under the water between the broken boards of the dock. She watched Dudley regain his composure. "I'm sorry. That man abuses his authority. He'll pay for that one day."

"That doesn't surprise me," Poppy played along. "He's a bully. You have to get out of here, Dudley. I don't feel safe at the cottage when he comes around."

Dudley stared at her, in silence. And Poppy wondered if she had gone too far. *Was she not convincing to him?*

"He could lose his badge with a statement like that from a beautiful woman like you," Dudley stated. She still had him. His obsession with her was unhealthy and raw. If Poppy played this scenario right, he would bring himself down.

"I don't want to start trouble," she stated. "I just want answers. I can't remember. My memory may never come back. The doctors don't know for sure. Dudley, how did I end up in the water?"

He looked down. "We talked out there, and like so many times before — we connected," Dudley began to explain, and Poppy was disgusted by him. Her mind flashed to his hands strangling her. And those same hands grabbing the hood on her sweatshirt, forcing it over her face, and shoving her by her head underneath the surface of the ocean. "That dock, it's old, it's brittle. There's probably been no upkeep at all since you stood on it as a child. You fell through. Two of the wood slabs just gave away underneath your feet. It happened so fast, I tried Poppy, I tried. I reached down for you. The water was just too cold for you. You sunk fast. You gave up from the hypothermia I guess. And then before I could make another frantic attempt to save you, the chief was on my back, cuffing me. He claimed I tried to drown you."

Poppy covered her hand over her mouth. She allowed tears to come to her eyes. She was crying because of what he had done to her out there, and how the outcome could have been altogether different for her — *if not for Kirk.*

"You're trembling," he said, as he took two steps away from the window now.

"I'm scared. I don't believe that you would ever try to hurt me like that. I don't want to accept it anyway." Poppy really was scared. Fearful of what she was doing right now. And terrified that he would take more steps closer to her in that locked room.

"Of course I wouldn't," he spoke softly. "This confirms that the chief is hell-bent on taking my freedom," Dudley scoffed.

"Do you know why?" she asked him outright, and Dudley stayed silent. "His wife died. He lost his wife, just like you did, Dudley. I know that can change a man. I saw what it did to you. Your grief pained me. Maybe the chief is just lashing out at you or anyone he can. His wife has been gone awhile, I think, unlike yours. You already are handling your loss like a man. You know how to move on."

"Yes. Thank you. Yes," Dudley repeated, staring at her from across the room. "I wanted to move on with you. We still can. Wait for me. This mess has to play out sooner or later."

"It will," Poppy told him. "I'll be by your side for it. I'll give a statement to the police. I'll tell them I remember what happened to me, I'll play by your story. I trust you, Dudley."

Trust. He appeared to have bought it. In the next room, Kirk had not moved from the other side of the wall. The play by play in his ear was like a movie where every moment counted. Look away and you'll miss something big.

"You would do that for me?" he asked.

"For us," she replied, and he took two more steps toward her. *Oh God. Oh God.* "You have to know something first. You have to accept me for my faults," Poppy begged. She was going full speed ahead with this notion to make herself out to be undeserving of him. And she prayed to God he would fall for it. Kirk, on the other hand, felt as if she was grasping at straws, but from what he could hear — it may have been working. "I cannot blindside you. I won't take the risk of you finding out something about me and then not wanting me. Your rejection would kill me." *Your rejection would kill me.* How ironic was that? Poppy's rejection of him had almost gotten her killed!

"I don't understand. You are the most pure and honest woman I've ever met." That wasn't exactly true. Dudley had also believed that about his own wife. And perceived it about the chief's wife, too. He looked for, desperately sought out, women of that character.

"I told you about my ex-husband. His betrayal sent me over the edge," Poppy had not planned this. It was impromptu, but worthy of a good shot. She had nothing else to go on. And she was too far into this with him to back up, or change gears now. "Remember I said that I followed my husband to a funeral home?" Dudley didn't react, he just continued to stare, so Poppy carried on with her story. And that's exactly what it was, *a story.* "His mistress was dead, in a coffin — because I put her there." Dudley's eyes widened, and Poppy felt strong in her words. "She was killed in a car accident. It was a one-car related incident, covered up so well. I ran her off the road, to her death."

"Oh Jesus," Dudley spoke. He wasn't shocked, or repulsed though. It was as if she lit a fire inside of him. It was as if one criminal to another, swapping stories of their transgressions, had given him an instant high. "Didn't that feel great, I mean just amazing, to slam your foot on the gas pedal and steer strategically so as you forced another car off the roadway? It's road rage at its best. The fear, the panic in the other person's eyes is laughable." *Holy smokes. This was it. You're almost there, Poppy.*

Kirk felt a similar rage behind the wall. That was his wife who was filled with fear and panic. And that son a bitch deserved to be ripped apart, limb by limb. Kirk had to contain himself. Poppy may not have been on the path to get a recorded confession from Dudley regarding her own attempted murder, but she was so close to getting to the truth about how Dudley ended the life of the chief's wife.

Poppy forced herself to laugh at what he described. It was far from funny though. It was sad and sick, and every other adjective that would make this man the most awful person alive in her eyes. "Dudley, that bitch deserved to die," Poppy said, referring to Reed's mistress. Dudley, however, didn't get her drift, he didn't pick up on how she was speaking of her husband's lover. It was as if he was in a trance, and focused on his former lover. The chief's late wife.

"Yes, she did. She didn't want me anymore. She made promises that she did not keep. She was going back to the chief." *There, yes, there!* Dudley implicated himself in a murder. "I ran her fucking ass off the roadway. She was killed instantly. Some things just work out, you know?"

Poppy sucked in a deep breath through her nostrils. "I know," she said, and she was only thinking of one thing. *This mess she had gotten herself into was finally over.*

Dudley stepped toward her. Panic immediately rose to her chest. "You are not a bad person, not in my eyes. Your coming here today was not what I expected. God, you're so beautiful. I wanted you to be mine, and you were…but then you pulled away. I can't handle that, Poppy. I can accept what you just told me. We are one in the same, now more than I ever thought." Poppy forced a smile, and then she watched Dudley reach for her. His hand touched the side of her face. It's what he did before he pulled her into a kiss. She had been there twice before with him. The very first time, she responded. The second time, she was repulsed. And now, this time, she had to pretend. She had to will herself numb just to get through it. The confession was solid. Their mission was accomplished. She closed her eyes and thought to herself, *Kirk, please come in now. End this. Save me from him.*

Dudley was close. Entirely too close for comfort. She opened her eyes and his lips were nearly touching hers. And then she felt both of his hands grip her throat. Tight, and then much tighter.

"You bitch," he said to her through clenched teeth. "I can see it in your eyes now. You didn't mean any of it. They may

lock me up forever, but I'll kill you first." Poppy screamed at
the very top of her lungs, but he was quick to completely cut off
her air flow. She grabbed his wrists, but she wasn't strong
enough to fight him off. Again. She had absolutely no air, and
not enough strength to overcome his grip. She fought, but that
only triggered him to strengthen his grip. Her knees gave out,
and just as she fell to the floor, the door to that room of insanity
was kicked in. Kirk charged Dudley and threw him down onto
the floor. Behind him was the orderly, the young black man
who escorted her into that room, and he was relentlessly aiming
a gun. The Daybreak Clubhouse obviously wasn't his actual day
job.

Poppy watched Kirk forcefully tighten a pair of handcuffs around Dudley's wrists. Face down on the tile floor,
Poppy could not see his reaction. She watched Kirk grab him by
the back of his hair. Those brown curls were nearly yanked
from his scalp. Dudley had not said a word. Not even a grunt.
But Kirk did. "You are a useless human being who preys on
innocent women. Hear my words. Remember them. You are
going to listen to them again and again in a court of law, when I
take the stand to put you away for the rest of your life. And
maybe, just maybe, the boys in prison will tear you apart, limb
by limb — just for fun. I can't. I value my life, my career, my
freedom, entirely too much." But, for his wife, he had wanted to
stoop to Dudley's level and end a life. He loathed Dudley
Connors and everything he had ever done to harm the woman
he once called his wife, and also the courageous woman in the
room with him now.

"Rookie," Poppy heard Kirk say to the young cop in their
presence, wearing medical scrubs but packing heat. "Nice job

today. Get him outta here. Show this useless asshole to his new home. Décor will be iron bars."

Poppy never looked at Dudley as he was forcefully guided out of there. She had gone from bent on her knees, to her bottom on the floor. Kirk made his way down to her. But by now she couldn't look at him either. Her face was in her hands just as she was overcome with emotion. She started to cry, and he enveloped her so fast into his arms that she had to catch her breath in between sobs. "It's over. Dammit, it's finally over," he repeated as he held her close, touched the hair on the back of her head, and she thought she heard him choke on a sob.

When she released herself from his embrace, he lifted her chin to get a closer look at her. He put his fingers on her tender neck. "You okay? How bad did he hurt you?" The faint bruises previously on her neck were now accompanied by fresh red marks.

"What took you so long to get in here?" she teased him.

He grinned. "What possessed you to botch our plan?" he lightheartedly chided her, but he partly meant it. Her risk could have cost them everything if Poppy had not been so convincing. Or if Dudley had not been so consumed with his obsession for her.

"It worked, didn't it?" she stated, as a matter of fact.

"Absolutely. You're a natural. I think we should sign you up for the academy," Kirk laughed. "But first, let's get the hell out of here. You need to get checked out at the hospital."

"No, no hospital. I'm good. Good as new. Bruises heal," Poppy stated, adamantly.

"You're tough. And certainly the bravest woman I've ever met," Kirk smiled at her. He was so damn relieved nothing had happened to her in there today. He promised Poppy she would be safe. And, for a matter of seconds, when he was on the other side of that door, the chief had terror running through his entire being. Saving her was suddenly the only thing that mattered to him.

"Tough *enough*," Poppy responded. *Yes, she finally was.*

Chapter twenty-five

The December air temperature on island was at its freezing point. Thirty-two degrees. Poppy didn't even care to know what the wind chill was out there on that beach. She was bundled in her winter white down jacket, with the hood covering her head. This time, her feet were not bare. Snow boots in the sand were an interesting mishmash, she giggled to herself. She had been there on island and at the cottage for six weeks now. More than ever, she wanted to stay indefinitely. Boston, however, would call her home for special events in the lives of her children and grandchildren. She was certain of that.

The matching winter white gloves on her hands held five roses, all of various colors. She fingered for the green rose first. A green rose was a rarity. She had to special order it from the florist of Oak Bluffs. The color of a green rose depicted life, abundant growth, and constant renewal of life and energy. That was for Bobby. Her little brother who, despite the end his life at eleven years old, had lived on as all of those things — inside of Poppy's heart. She tossed it into the frigid waters of the Atlantic Ocean, and she watched it be swept away by the tide. She stared long and as far as her eyes could see.

She grasped for the white rose next. It was the purist of the colors. It meant innocence, purity, and charm. It could also symbolize remembrance. That rose was for her mother. The mother she respected and admired prior to her brother's death. The mother that, despite everything, Poppy had loved and learned from. Poppy tossed her white rose high up into the air before it reached the water. In the end, her mother had led her back there, to the cottage she now called her own. For whatever reason, Julie Blare had not been able to share her grief, or her method of healing. Poppy understood that now, after discovering her mother had actually been back there. She accepted what was. It was the only way to move on.

A traditional red rose was next. *Who else would that be for?* The only man she ever truly loved. Reed Brennan was still very much a part of this earth, but his existence in Poppy's life as a husband, lover, and best friend had ceased. A red rose also reflected beauty and perfection. That's what Reed had given her in both of her daughters. CeCe and Tealy. As she had told Reed on the dock of that very beach, she would always love him. The red rose was stubborn to land in the water as the wind had taken it for endless seconds. Poppy laughed to herself. *Leave it to Reed.* A standout, defiant rose which chose to go against the odds for as long as possible — before finally accepting defeat. The wind eventually calmed and the rose hit the water. There was no anger or bitterness in Poppy's heart as she said goodbye to the red rose.

Next to last, she held an orange rose in her hand. It was another color of specialty order. Orange roses were uncommon, but the meaning behind the color was the perfect choice in Poppy's mind. Enthusiasm, desire, and excitement. Those were the emotions Poppy felt first when she met Dudley Connors. First impressions were not always made of truth. Poppy discovered that in the most trying way. Even still, Dudley had taught her something invaluable. The orange rose also was said to evoke energy. And that was what Dudley had ultimately done for Poppy. He stirred and he surfaced the fighter in her. All along, she had been a woman who wouldn't give up, wouldn't be crushed. She finally recognized that about herself now. *So long, orange rose.*

The final rose in her hand was a novelty rose. No one novelty rose was the same. They all were uniquely colored, and multi-colored. This one was the combination of a yellow, pink, and white rose with a red tip. The meanings were friendship, gratitude, and falling in love. Poppy never tossed the novelty rose into the ocean. She turned around to face the wind, which earlier had shown mercy at her back, as she walked up to the cottage.

On the boardwalk, he stood there in his full police uniform. "We need to get you inside where it's warm," Kirk told her, and then he looked down at the one rose left in her gloved hand. He recalled her telling him of how she would toss four roses into the ocean — for who they represented in her life. "One more?" he asked, perplexed.

"For you," Poppy said. "It's a novelty rose."

"Yeah? I'm not really a flower kind of guy," he smiled. "Explain the colors to me."

"It means first passionate kiss," she broke into a smile. She never could keep a straight face when she fibbed.

"Seriously?" he asked her. He savored the fact that they were just kids, twelve and fourteen, at the time. A connection. A piece of their history, his and hers, had been tossed back into their lives all of these years later.

Poppy shook her head, laughing. "No, not really. A novelty rose has a twist of messages actually. It's fun. It's friendship. It's gratitude. And, if there are red tips on the rose," Poppy fingered those on this particular rose, "it also can symbolize falling in love."

"That's my new favorite kind of rose," Kirk smiled, as he pulled her into his arms and kissed her passionately. It wasn't the first kiss between them. That kiss was more than four decades ago on the very same beach. This wasn't going to be their last kiss either.

ABOUT THE AUTHOR

I could talk endlessly about the characters I've created (in fifteen different books). But when I'm asked to talk about myself, I stare at a flashing curser on my wordless computer screen.

My characters are not me, but they are a part of me. I've felt much of what they have. I think we all have. That's why, I believe, my readers can relate to the stories I write. It's not just me. It's the craft of storytellers in general. They have a way of reaching us, helping us escape, making us feel, and (hopefully) giving us hope.

In this novel, Begin Again, the main character was lost and alone when she arrived on Martha's Vineyard. There was no moment of inspiration for me to write the story. Instead, it was the truth that we all live in an unsettled state of mind at some point in our lives. What comes of that — or how we hold our heads above water during trying and changing times — is entirely up to us.

Poppy, in her time of sadness and despair, eventually found her strength. It had been inside of her all along, she just hadn't credited herself enough. Maybe you've overcome something in your life that you never thought possible. Perhaps you're struggling through it now. Or, it could be just around the bend. Life works that way sometimes. Whatever the scenario, my wish for you is to find your strength (just like Poppy did). Remember, it's already inside of you. Just reach for it.

As always, thank you for reading!

love,

Lori Bell